A Killer
in the
Rye

D0181054

Also by Delia Rosen

A BRISKET A CASKET

ONE FOOT IN THE GRAVY

A Killer
in the
Rye

Delia Rosen

KENSINGTON PUBLISHING CORP.

http://www.kensingtonbooks.com

KENSINGTON BOOKS are published by

Kensington Publishing Corp.
119 West 40th Street
New York, NY 10018

ISBN-13: 978-0-7582-4172-6
ISBN-10: 0-7582-4172-0

First Mass Market Printing: December 2012

10 9 8 7 6 5 4 3 2 1

Printed in the United States of America

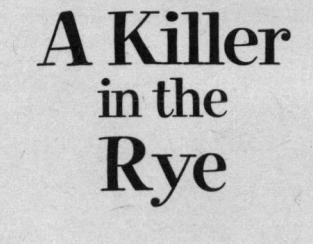

A Killer
in the
Rye

Chapter 1

"I'm confused," Dani Spicer said through the ring in her upper lip. "What's this about not usin' pig? You're afraid I won't *crush her?*"

We were at the counter, preparing to open Murray's Pastrami Swami Kosher Delicatessen for the day. I looked at the new girl, who was reviewing the menu for the last time before her big day. Sweet Dani, innocent Dani, twentysomething Dani, who had never been out of Davidson County. Blue-eyed, nose-also-pierced, my-middle-name-really-is-Petunia Dani.

"What I said," I said, "is it's not *kosher.* That's a kind of healthy eating."

"Ko-shaw," she repeated carefully.

"Sounds like an Indian name, right?" asked Luke, who was washing dishes in the kitchen, behind the heat lamps. I didn't bother looking at him. That would only encourage him.

"It's a very old tradition," I said. "It comes from a time when the Jewish people were concerned about trichinosis, a parasitic disease that comes from pork. All they knew was that when they ate food from pigs, they got sick. So they made dietary rules to protect themselves."

"Whoa," Dani said, as though she'd enjoyed a revelation. "Is that why so many Jewish men have beards?"

"I don't follow," I said, expecting the worst.

"Because they're so healthy, they live longer," she said.

Oy vey. It's hard to find help these days, never mind good help. I'd gotten used to running the deli with my trusty skeleton crew, but word of mouth in the Music City travels fast, and I can't complain about a boomin' business, can I?

Jeez. Did I really just say "boomin'" without a *g* in my head? Was I at risk of becoming a real Southerner, like Dani?

New York City seemed so far away, like a life I only once dreamed of having. Lately I'd felt like I was a divorced thirtysomething-year-old woman, which I was, who ran a Jewish deli I'd inherited, which I did. I had two cats, who suddenly wanted very little to do with me when I was home, a boyfriend who was busier locking up bad guys than hooking up with me, and a new girl who—

"Ohhh," Dani went on as the epiphanies continued. "*Kosher*. Like those jars with the pickles in 'em?"

"Exactly," I said.

"Those are the best tastin' ones, and you're sayin' they're healthy eatin', too?"

"They're pretty healthy, yeah," I told her.

Dani's large blue eyes sparkled with more excitement than I had ever seen anyone muster when speaking of dill pickles. I wondered if she had glowed with the same enthusiasm when she'd worked at an all-girl car wash or as a dog walker, because, according to the application she'd filled out, "I seen J Lo do it in a movie, and it seemed real glam."

She'd seen J Lo do it. And it seemed glam.

I couldn't help but wonder why slender, five-foot-high, blond-haired Dani was the one to walk through my deli door this morning, at the exact moment when my dishwasher broke—with the repair guy on vacation—Newt dropped eight pounds of brisket on the floor, my inventory and order guy suddenly resigned, and business had, happily, reached a point where my tidy little staff couldn't handle it. Not without a full-scale revolt. Again. I had never thought I was a fatalist, but I hired her then and there. Which was not a ringing endorsement of fatalism. Though it was partly Luke's fault. He encouraged me. She wasn't brilliant, but she was bright, a radiant little looker. In this business, that mattered.

Thomasina Jackson is the mother hen of my late uncle Murray's deli, a hostess and no-nonsense, genuine Southern lady and God fearer who probably knows ten times as much about the deli as I do.

"I thought that with the nickname Nashville Katz, it had to be, like, a music place. You know . . . Katz? Cats . . . meow?" Dani said.

"Yes, that's sort of the joke of the name," I told her.

"Okay, well, that's what I want to do—music. Like Lady Gaga. And like Luke. I want to be on *American Idol.*"

Luke beamed at the mention of his name juxtaposed with one of his heroes.

"How did you know my nickname if you've never been here?" I asked.

She shrugged. "I dunno. I heard it somewhere."

I didn't press.

Thom said, "So tell me, honey, why did you stay when you found out we serve 'just deli' and not 'just dance'?"

Dani smiled. "That was funny, Thom."

"Thom rules!" Luke offered.

"Thank you both."

"I have to say, I'm kinda glad to hear we all don't serve pigs," Dani said. "My middle name is the same as a pig's."

"Dig it," Luke said. "She was named after Porky Pig's gal pal."

"My mom really likes cartoons," she said.

I felt like I was trapped in an SNL version of *Lord of the Flies*.

"But gettin' back to the big Dani openin' day here," the girl said, "I want to make sure I got it, y'all." While she spoke, she had brought up Wikipedia on her cell phone. "*Kosher* means that all flyin' 'n' creepin' things are considered ritually unclean. That's accordin' to both Leviticus and Deuteronomy."

At least she could pronounce her Bible names. I had to give her that. She probably learned them before she could count—which I was hoping she could do.

"Leviticus lists four creepin' exceptions," she went on.

"CreepLeeches!" Luke interjected with a cheer.

"What?" Dani said.

"Let's hear it for my cousin Zach and his band! *Yeahhh*."

He looked up from the sink, to which he was giving a morning disinfecting; then, cowed by glares from the rest of us, he looked back down. Luke was referring to the band name on the side of the van we'd borrowed for a recent off-site catering debacle, the CreepLeeches.

Throughout what I hoped would not become a morning ritual with my new hire, Newt, our college-dropout cook, went about his business, as did my waitresses—

sorry, *waitstaff,* as Raylene and A.J. both insisted I call them—who were setting tables.

"With regard to animals," Dani continued, as though everyone were listening, "Deuteronomy and Leviticus say that anything which chews the cud and has a cloven hoof is ritually clean." She looked up. "That makes sense. Like the devil, right? He has cloven hooves? But animals that only chew the cud or only have cloven hooves are not. Wait. What?"

"You don't have to worry about that," Thom assured her. "That all gets sorted out somewhere else."

"Good, because I don't even know what cud is," Dani admitted.

"Okay! That's enough, kiddies," I said. "Just so you know, phones are not permitted at the counter."

"Why? What if I get a call?"

"You won't, if you want to work here. And, Luke, I'll promote you tomorrow if you manage to keep up with the dishes all day."

Thom gave me one of her "Lighten up" looks, which was fair enough. The new girl was making me nuts, and she didn't want me taking it out on customers. I was still adjusting to the Southern way of doing things—always polite and attentive, not to mention slooooow—and I had to fight the urge to get them in and out like it was the number two train at rush hour.

"Patience," Thom's gentle eyes and smile said. "Remember how long it would take you to make a sandwich when you first started? Learning to pile pastrami and cole slaw on rye bread without having it fall apart?"

I'd still be serving three customers an hour if Thom hadn't shown me the ropes. At least the girl was into it. Her head was in the game.

I went over to A.J.

"When is A.J. Two coming back?" I asked her platinum-blond beanpole of a mother.

"She's back. Got home from West Virginia University last night."

A.J. Two was A.J.'s daughter. We numbered her to tell them both apart. The numeric designation made Luke laugh. He didn't understand why we just didn't call her Poop. He was a child.

"She going to be able to fill in?" I leaned closer. "Maybe help Dani out if she needs it?"

"Her dad 'n' me won't have her sittin' around textin' boys all day," A.J. said. "I'll work up her schedule. We can use her as a swing."

I got my keys from the office.

"Hey, kid." Luke chin motioned for Dani to join him at the sink. "You want to learn how to wash dishes?"

"Not really," Dani said. "I've got to keep my head in this kosher game. And, like, that wasn't in the job description."

"There are a lot of *perks* that aren't in the job description, either." Luke's green eyes looked down at Dani, the right one squinted ever so slightly.

"Did you just wink at me?" Dani asked.

"Totally," he replied.

She giggled, then got serious again. That was a great quality for a waitstaffer—being able to take a surprise of some kind, roll with it, and get back in the race. And for the record, now that I thought of it fresh, *waitstaffer* is a word that sounds like something you'd wear in the Swiss Alps. I would never get used to it.

I went to unlock the front door. There were already three women outside. Plus, the coffee-and-bagel crowd would be here shortly.

"Hey, y'all!" Luke called. "Before the rush, I just want to announce that I have a show tonight and Sunday night at the Five Spot. I'll put you on the list, if you like. I mean, you did say you liked music."

"You still need a list with an empty room?" Thomasina muttered before greeting the three women at the door. Thom was Old South and not the biggest fan of Luke's own band, the Gutter Crickets. None of us knew if Thomasina had ever gotten past the band's name and had actually given them a listen.

"Glad you heard that, too, Thomasina," Luke said. "I'm puttin' you on that list!"

"I'll be there Sunday night if you come to church with me Sunday."

"I will," Dani said.

"Dani, just focus on today," I warned.

"And beware the all-knowing Mama Thoma," Luke said, adding his own warning.

"To work, people," I ordered.

Thomasina showed the three women to their table, and Dani, proud in her new white outfit and clean apron, went over when they were seated. This was her first flight. It was also the first *first* flight I got to witness. All the other staffers had been here when I arrived.

A.J. sidled over. "You sure the new girl's gonna cut it?"

"I'm never sure of anything but prices rising," I said. "But I hope for the best."

"Cool beans," she said.

The three ladies were regulars. They came in once a week or so and always sat close to the counter. Inevitably, they inspected everything, from the food and drinks to the decor and cleanliness of the front windows; showed their obvious distaste; then sucked down whatever was in front of them. Most establishments in the nearby Arcade, an alley of restaurants and specialty shops, knew these women as the "Repeat Returner Club." They'd shop for hours at a time, moving painstakingly slow while asking questions and finally flashing frequent shopper or diner discounts before purchasing. Then they'd return the merchandise later that week. At least my goods were not returnable.

"What can I get you ladies today?" Dani asked cheerily.

"Well, what are y'all's specials today?" asked the leader, Big Red.

"They would be the special items listed on the board behind me, ma'am."

"I didn't ask you to point 'em out to me. I asked you what they were."

My brain said, *Crap.* It was beginning. I was standing behind the counter, at the cash register. I decided not to step in. Yet.

"Are you new here?" Big Red asked.

"Why, yes, ma'am," Dani replied.

"Do you have the Preferred Diners Club set up yet?" barked Brownie, the second in command. "I spoke to your manager about that last week."

"I will be just *ever* so happy to check on that for you, ma'am."

"Well, don't do that yet," purred the catlike Blondie. "First take our drink order. Didn't they tell you that?"

"Yes, ma'am. Drinks followed by pickles."

"Did they tell you not to put your thumb in the pickle dish?" Big Red inquired.

"No they did not, and it's a good thing you pointed that out."

"Ahem," Blondie said. "We would like two unsweetened iced teas with Sweet'N Low on the side—make sure it's Sweet'N Low—and one Diet Coke."

"Got that," Dani said. "Would you like a lemon or lime with that beverage?"

"Did I ask for one?" Blondie said.

"You did not," Dani agreed. "I thought, with so much on your mind, like pickle thumbs, you may have forgotten."

The women glared at her.

"At what point do you tell us the specials?" Brownie demanded.

"Ma'am, I will recite them to you just as soon as I finish writing and you finish talking."

And I thought, *Time to step in.*

"Dani, why don't you go get started on the drinks?" I interrupted, crossing the near empty dining area.

"Our specials today are corned beef hash with two eggs, the Egg Lover's Sandwich, which is a western omelet on your choice of toast, and our classic matzoh brei. What would you ladies like?" I said.

"What I would *like* is for you to give that new girl a talking to." Blondie frowned.

"Oh, I forgot. You also get a choice of home fries or fruit salad with your meal."

Rule number one in dealing with the insane or the childish: divert their attention and ignore bad behavior.

"I'll take a small fruit salad," Big Red said, starting it off. "Then the Egg Lover's Sandwich on rye, and I want home fries."

"Very good," I said, then braced myself. "But we had a run on rye and are out. We have wheat, sourdough—"

"I *do not* believe this!" Blondie huffed. "A deli without rye!"

"We had a problem with—"

"Why don't we just go to IHOP?" Big Red asked the others.

For show. It sounded like they'd used this shtick before. Dani arrived with the drinks just in time to watch it play out.

"I wanted Diet Coke," whined Blondie after sipping it.

"But that is Diet—"

"It is regular Coke," Blondie said, draining half the glass.

"Dani, just go get another."

"Wow, that's so not kosher," she muttered, turning. The women gazed after her. As if she felt their eyes on her, Dani turned and smiled and said, "Definition number two."

Good girl, I thought with a private little smile.

Thom approached from her perch—no, really, there was a picture of a fish on the stool—and looked over her glasses at the women, unbemused.

"Nash, phone for you," Thom publicized, using my nickname. "It's McCoy's Bakery."

"Thom, can you just finish this up for me?"

Her look grew even more unbemused, which I didn't think was possible. "Yes, I can. You were giving directions to IHOP?"

I could hear the ladies protesting about having "three servers in three minutes, each ruder than the one before."

I like that, I thought as I made my way behind the counter. Servers *is a much better word than* waitstaffer. I picked up my office phone and pressed the blinking button next to line one. "This is Gwen."

"Hi, Gwen. This is Brenda Silvio," said the gruff-sounding woman on the other end of the line. Brenda and her husband, Joe, were the co-owners of McCoy's Bakery. I knew her husband only by phone, and I didn't know Brenda at all. "I understand there's an issue with your order?"

"Yes, Brenda. I haven't received it."

"Okay, I'm seeing here that your extra bread order was put in at one a.m., by telephone. You left it with the night staff."

"That's correct."

"And you wanted same-day delivery."

"I suppose yes, technically. One a.m. is the same day as today. But that was six hours ago."

"Well, we don't do that here."

"'That' being what?"

"Same day. The night man should have told you that."

"He did. And I told him that it was okay if I didn't get it until late in the day, because we wouldn't start preparing the sandwiches until after hours."

"I understand," Brenda said. "But I can't get the bread to you until tomorrow, late morning. The way our ovens are set up, with schedules, I can't add your fifteen extra loaves until after today's regular run."

"You're saying a little over a dozen loaves of bread will throw off your entire operation?"

"No. I'm saying I won't let fifteen extra loaves throw off my operation."

Nashville was sinking, and New York was rising. I had to give it a little free rein, just to keep it in shape.

"Brenda, I order bread three times a week, every week, on Mondays, Wednesdays, and Fridays. The deli has been doing that for years. I told your man that I knew this order was unusual due to a special event I have tomorrow. I said I know it's not my usual day but that I wanted everything fresh—"

"Our bread is always fresh!"

"That's right, or we wouldn't be having this conversation," I said. "I told him I wanted everything fresh and high quality, which is why I didn't just run over to the grocery store and grab what I need. He said he didn't think that would be any problem at all. I told him if he couldn't do it to let me know so I could buy from Sam's in Brentwood—who said he could handle the order. That was the last I heard until now. So here's the deal, Brenda.

I need that order. If I don't get it, I will move my business to Sam's."

"Excuse me, but why did you wait until today to place your order?"

"Fair question, Brenda. The answer is, someone on my staff was supposed to have placed the order. He forgot, probably because he was too busy setting up another business opportunity and quitting."

"I see here that would be Mr. Siegel."

"That's right. Richard Siegel, my accountant and inventory control wizard."

Siegel was one of my uncle's last hires, someone he met in a steam room. The previous month, Dick had arrived in Nashville to work at a local subprime lender just before it went under. That was on the heels of having been given a semi-golden parachute from Owen-Wister-Storey in New York. So he went to work for Murray. As soon as I came down here, he started showing up at the deli, usually before closing, and hitting on me. That flopped for two reasons: I believe in the separation of church and state, of work and private life, and he wasn't my type. Physically, he was fine, but I didn't want another New York Jewish male with a Wall Street background.

He didn't take rejection well and started working from home in his bathrobe, running everything by computer. Then, starting a month ago, orders were getting placed incorrectly or not at all. On purpose, I suspect, because Dick reveled in schadenfreude, the German concept of deriving joy from the misery of others. I remember him sitting in the office we used to share, cackling gleefully on the phone because friends there told him that Owen-Wister-Storey was getting parcels meant for the unwashed masses of the other OWS—Occupy Wall Street. The firm subsequently changed its name to Virginian Capital, after one of the partners' mothers. It was immediately picketed by African American members of OWS, who insisted its "stars" logo replicated the Confederate battle flag. Dick claimed to have left the deli to work as an e-trader, investing funds for local widows. The whole thing had the reek of *The Producers,* but, thankfully, it was not my concern.

"So it would appear that Mr. Siegel is the one at fault here, not us," Brenda said conclusively.

"We are actually in agreement there, Brenda," I replied. "The question is, what are you going to do about it?"

I was starting to get heated, like I used to get with my ex-husband, Phil, especially toward the end of my "blissful" few years as Mrs. Silver. We'd get four sentences into a conversation and it would become an argument, no matter what the topic was. Now that I think of it, we once argued about bread, burnt toast, which happened because we were arguing about something else. And usually, two sentences after those four sentences, I was threatening to walk. Like I was now.

Brenda—whom I really didn't know, and I wasn't sure I wanted to—apparently hadn't heard anything I'd said.

"Ma'am," Brenda told me—in the same patiently insincere tone of voice I'd just used on the Repeat Returners, which didn't sit so well—"ma'am, I'm going to have to talk this over with my husband, Joe, who is the manager. But I think that this is too-short notice."

In business, repetition is corporatespeak for "You're never going to get what you want." I know. I did that for years, when I worked in finance.

"Brenda, let me take one final stab at this. I just had a tough time with three other women who didn't seem to understand English, so I'm going to make this simple. I get my order, or you lose my business."

"There is no need for threats, Ms. Katz—"

"Apparently there is. Did you not understand that I need the damn bread?"

"Or harsh language."

I was about to unleash some harsher language when I heard someone say good-bye to her on the other end of the line.

Oh, thought I. *This is about the shift ending. Overtime.*

"I'll tell you what, Brenda," I said. "How about you put the brakes on one or two guys in your baking staff leaving? I'll pay for the bread and the overtime. Will that solve the problem?"

Brenda thought for a moment. "That will cost you an extra seventy-three dollars and ten cents."

"A figure arrived at how?" I asked.

"It's a random but fair number that just came to me," she said.

"That's a lot of bread, but I need the bread," I said, wondering if I'd ever have a chance to use that line again. "And I'm willing to accept that we screwed up on our end, so I'll assume, just this once, the extra expense."

I wasn't typically into appeasement, but this had gone on long enough, and truth be told, I hadn't contacted Sam's. And store-bought rye just wasn't going to cut it. Not for a meeting of the people who were supposed to select the Best of Nashville in my profession.

"I'll tell you what," Brenda said. "Hold on while I make a quick call."

"Sure." I held on. Could it be that my willingness to accede to her needs actually got her to show some compassion? Did such yin and yang actually exist in the business universe?

She came back, sounding light, almost buoyant.

"Ms. Katz, if you're willing to give me a few extra hours, and come in a little early tomorrow, I will get it to you before the usual rounds. Joe will bring it to you personally, fresh from the oven."

"Bright and early?"

"Before five a.m."

"For certain? You'll have it here before I open, waiting for me on your little plastic pallets?"

"Still hot," Brenda said.

"Deal," I said and hung up. Before she could change her mind

As I stepped from my cramped office and returned to the deli counter, I saw Luke frozen with a look of horror, Dani all blue eyes, and Thom with her hands crossed over her chest and eyebrows raised. I turned my eyes toward the table of the Repeat Returners as they shook their heads slowly from side to side, sipping on their drinks.

I looked over at Newt in the kitchen.

"I didn't close my door, did I?"

Chapter 2

I had a date that night. I went to a movie with Detective Grant Daniels, whom I helped solve a real murder at a murder mystery party I catered. It was our first catering gig. Naturally, there had to be a homicide. But my uncle used to say, "Wherever there's a loss, there's a gain," and Grant was it.

Sort of.

Physically, we were a perfect match. Intellectually, he was not like the NYU professor I fell hard for when I was a student, or even Phil, who had an IQ of 120, despite a complete lack of self-awareness. But Grant was pretty sharp and had a lot of Southern graces.

He was also on call 24/7, and that was a pain. Especially because more crime happened at night, when I was in need of companionship and R & R. Not that I was a total day at the beach, either. Phil had left me pretty scarred, since I apparently couldn't measure up to his mother, and after a day of being surrounded by needy customers and almost as needy staff, I didn't have a lot left to give.

The movie was so-so—I am not a fan of Meryl Streep, even though it was sweet of Grant to think I'd want to see her as Margaret Thatcher—and we decided to stay in our respective places since I had to be up real early to make sure the bread was there.

He dropped me at my door, a forty-year-old colonial my late father and his brother had shared on the unfortunately named Bonerwood Drive.

"See you tomorrow?" he asked.

"Sure," I said.

"Sure?" he said, wounded. "Not hell yeah!"

"Hell yeah!" I said.

He frowned. "I know, you're tired."

"Beat."

He cupped my face, kissed me softly on the lips. It was a short kiss. We didn't have time to get overstimulated.

"You are surely different from any woman I have ever known," he said.

"I hope that's a good thing."

"So far," he said.

He left with a stiff-armed wave, like a politician getting into a campaign bus. I had an unhappy feeling, but I didn't know why.

I woke fifteen minutes before my alarm went off. The earliest rays of the sun were shining through the crack in the drapes, pinkishly illuminating the flyaway cat hair dancing through the air. I looked down toward the bottom of the bed to see the two wide-eyed, hungry culprits.

"Okay, I'm up. Let's get you fed."

After emptying a cup of kibble into each of their bowls, I stepped from my cotton robe into a hot shower. Today was going to be great. I could feel it. Sure, the day before had been stressful and I hadn't entirely been myself, but today was the day after the storm, the day the sun came out and the earth smelled clean.

The drive downtown was easy as baking apple pie. That's a wonderful thing about Nashville: there's never any traffic any time of day, even during football games and music events. And that morning every light turned green for me, and there was no line at my favorite Starbucks, inside the neighboring Hotel Indigo. Even though I often made my favorite coffee at home and served coffee at the deli, I couldn't break my Starbucks routine when I wanted a latte. Okay, habit. Old New York addictions are like New York cockroaches. They just don't die.

I parked in my usual spot in the public garage, said my hello to Randy, the parking attendant, then rounded the corner and walked past the Arcade, with its cafés, shops, and salons, where I sometimes sneak off for lunch. I just say that I'm running over to the post office there. One can eat only so much deli food on a daily basis. As a result, I'd gotten pretty tight with all the café owners, since they also came to my deli to eat whatever I had fresh that day. And so our incestuous little culinary world goes round.

I stuck the gold key that I had seen my uncle Murray flip between his fingers countless times into the smooth lock and let myself in. In New York, if you own a great deli, you feel like part of a mob or something. A community that knows all kinds of secrets passed by oral tradition—and the occasional index card—through the generations. I was just starting to get that feeling here: being a part of something great, being talked about around town, and hopefully sealing the deal by being voted Best Mid-Range Restaurant in Nashville as soon as I'd successfully hosted the Best & Worst Committee luncheon that afternoon, which I'd won by lottery. It was sponsored by the local newspaper, a local radio station, the local chamber of commerce—in short, more locals than you find in the New York City subway system. As Murray used to say, "If you can't beat 'em, feed 'em," and I was about to do both very shortly.

I opened my office, set my grande vanilla latte on my desk, put my purse on Murray's old chair in the corner, and sat down at my desk to check the office voice mail before going out back to make sure the bread was there.

There was only one message. It was from McCoy's.

"Hey, this message is for Gwen Katz. Hello, Gwen. This is Joe Silvio from McCoy's Bakery. I just wanted to let you know that I'm on time to reach your place with your special delivery. It's about four fifty-five in the a.m. today, Thursday, and I should be there in approximately five minutes. I apologize if I'm later than expected, but you are the first stop on my route and I don't get to make up time by rushing. Thank you, and I'll see you in a few. Okay. Again, this is Joe Silvio from McCoy's Bakery. Bye now."

Okay, I thought with relief. *That was an hour ago. The bread's definitely here by now.*

I went to the back door that led out to my loading dock, which was just a simple concrete ramp designed to make loading and unloading a little easier. I used my key to disarm the emergency-exit push bar, then opened the door slowly, in case my bread had been placed right there.

It hadn't been. What was there, though, was the rear end of a bread truck with a smiley-faced French bread baguette and swirly black lettering that spelled McCoy's.

I propped open my heavy door with a cinder block that was there for that purpose. I had a class operation, top to bottom.

"Hello!" I called out.

It was very weird that Joe wasn't coming from the truck. The delivery truck's back door was partly open, and I could see straight through to the front, where the driver was sitting. Maybe he was on the phone? Or taking a power nap?

"Hello? Joe?"

I tried, and failed, to stop my brain from going into a rhyme my father used to say: "Hello, Joe. Whaddya know? I just got back from a vaudeville show!"

I walked down the ramp and stepped up into the back of the truck, ducking my head as I stopped a few feet from the driver. I noticed among the many paper bags of bread a large bunch marked with a black MD for Murray's Deli. I started gathering them in my arms.

"Joe?" I whispered as sweet as tea, in case he had dozed off. "Joe? Can we please just get this bread inside and let me sign for it? I have a really big day, as I'm sure you do, too, since I'm noticing a lot of places still haven't gotten their orders."

My foot skidded slightly on the floor as I lost my balance. Dropping the bags, I grabbed the back of the driver's side seat, letting the driver's head recline slightly as I did and revealing a pair of bulging eyes and a wide-open mouth. A large chunk of the right side of his neck was completely gone. I was still slipping, as if I were on an icy side street in Hell's Kitchen. I looked down at my feet in slow motion, trying hastily to put things together. My left foot was covered in blood and tissue. That was what I'd slid on.

The blood didn't look like ketchup, as it had when Hoppy Hopewell parachute jumped through Lolo's ceiling without the benefit of a silk canopy a few weeks back. This was more like a fine red wine, except for the blood that had mixed with some of the flour on his white apron, which created a Play-Doh-like paste. Blood had also pooled in the creases of his starched apron in the middle of his chest. Just underneath that pooling, stitched in swirly black thread, the name Joe was still visible. There was a bagged rye bread lying on the gear shift.

I must have dropped my keys, because I heard the loud ting of metal on metal, which caused me to jump backward. The top of my head bumped hard off the ceiling; my right hand shot out reflexively to keep my body upright as several of my fingertips smeared blood on the cold steel enclosure.

Instinctively, I looked out the back of the delivery truck and happened to see Luke standing just inside my deli's back door, his arm hanging weightlessly on the guitar strap slung over his shoulder. I covered my gaping mouth with my unsullied left hand. Neither of us moved.

"Is that real blood?" Luke asked.

"Yeah," I managed to reply.

"So, like, that guy in there is dead?"

"Y'know . . . I think so," I replied. "I didn't check. But enough of him is missing from his body."

"Man. The curse of Murray's."

"Don't go there," I warned. "Call nine-one-one."

"Anything you want me to say, other than we have a dead bread guy?"

"Tell them I found him like this when I went to pick up our order. And bring me paper towels when you're done."

"Hey, I don't think you should mess with a crime scene. I saw that on a TV show."

"It's for my hands," I told him. "I have some of his neck on me, I think."

"I'm on it," he said, which made no sense, because it seemed to take him forever to move.

I felt the walls closing in, and I started to get queasy, blood and scraps of ripped tissue and loaves of bread strewn about. The last threads of dawn had given way to

Nashville's blazing morning light. I was momentarily scared to move. I heard the bell on the deli's front door jingle.

"It's my pick today, boys and girls! I hope ya'll are ready for some Patsy Cline." It was the familiar and comforting voice of Thom approaching. Thank God and all His prophets. "Nash, what's going on with Luke? He looks like he's seen a . . . Oh, my dear Lord, *what?*"

I had my head crouched down slightly and saw her fill the open door. I just grimaced stupidly—it was either that or cry or scream or possibly both—as Thom reached in and pulled me from the truck, putting her arm around me right before I lost my legs. She sat me on the concrete ramp just outside the deli doors.

"Sit tight. I'm calling nine-one-one," Thom instructed.

"Luke is," I told her. I had the strangest urge to sneeze. I suppressed it.

"Okay, fine. I think Luke can manage that," Thom said. "You want something? Water?"

"I don't think I could get it down," I said, my nose still itching.

Luke showed up a few seconds later with a bottle of water and an entire case of paper towels.

"The cops are on the way, on the double," he said.

He tore into the thin plastic casing of the towels as he stared at the macabre tableau. He finally handed me a fresh roll, which I struggled to unspool. I felt like a fingerless cat, and I just started clawing at the glued seam to tear off a clean sheet, my bloody fingertips leaving streaks on the outermost layer.

"I've got to get my keys," I said stupidly.

"You leave 'em," Thom said, taking the roll of paper towels and wiping me as if I were three years old and had just made my first, messy Easy-Bake Cake. "We all have keys. Nobody's goin' back in there."

As I sat there, I heard the bell on the front door jingle again.

"Sorry I'm late, ya'll! I had a late-night line dancing session at the Crazy Horse."

"Luke, keep Dani in the front of the deli, please!" Thom yelled back.

"What?" Dani said, reaching the door. Her iPad earbuds literally flew out and down as her head snapped back. "Holy bejesus! That's, like, *so* nasty!"

From the mouths of babes, I thought. . . .

Chapter 3

"How was your gig last night?"

I was trying to make conversation with Luke, who was seated comfortably on a counter stool, eager-eyed and actually looking excited to be a part of the carnival that was a crime scene but used to be a deli.

"Eh, you know, Thursdays." Luke shrugged my question off. "Good thing the band was there buyin', or the bartender would have gone home empty-handed. I still think it's crappy that we don't get free drinks when we play, right?"

"Like you say, the bartender's got to earn a living."

I couldn't help but stare through Luke to where Thom was confidently going over the morning's gory details with the Nashville police. I wondered what it would take to make that woman break a sweat.

"We should totally do an open mic night here," Luke said, pressing. "I would be totally up for that."

The cops were in my office. I could see them behind the heat lamps, on the other side of the kitchen. It appeared the police were getting ready to wrap it up with Thom. Dani would be fast; she didn't really see anything. Worst-case scenario, the cops would be out in another half hour, and that'd put me only about an hour and a half behind schedule to prep for the big luncheon. I actually wondered how much of the bread would be salvageable.

"Would that be something you would consider?" Luke asked, bringing me back.

"Huh? Sorry, Luke. What?"

"Open mic night?"

"Um, could be," I said, without knowing what I'd possibly agreed to.

Thom came over. "How you holding up, Nash?"

"Oh, I'm fine. Just anxious to get this Best luncheon going, you know?"

"Well, darlin', we'll talk about it in just a minute," Thom said. "I'm running to the ladies' room. I'll be right back."

I watched as the police talked to Dani. She seemed her usual self. Maybe there was a value to a somewhat impervious skull. It kept out the good along with the bad.

"So I'm taking your 'could be' as a yes to open mic night!" Luke announced, pressing, his head cocked cutely sideways like that of an eager spaniel.

"Sure," I answered.

There must've been six police officers in all, three people in lab coats, and more yellow caution tape than in a haunted house. What had happened to my deli? Would anyone actually come in for the luncheon, assuming they were allowed inside?

Dani finished quickly. The police were officially beginning to wrap it up.

"Oh no, here comes the body," Luke gushed.

I saw it, too. *Right through my kitchen! Jerome H. Christ!*

Because the outside back of the shop was a crime scene, paramedics with the medical examiner's office wheeled the bagged body on a squeaky gurney past my counter and through my freshly set dining room, pushing tables and chairs out of the way, and then continued rolling the shimmying body bag through the jingling front door into the bright sunlight for all of gawking Nashville to see. I noticed Blondie out there. She'd probably eat most of a sandwich and then ask to be comped because she found blood on the crust.

An EMT accidentally flipped the sign to read OPEN and without missing a beat the crowd began to surge forward. They were met and pushed back by Thom, who flipped the sign back to CLOSED.

Mercifully, the coroner hadn't asked Joe's wife to come down and identify the body. That would be done at the morgue. I didn't think I could handle Brenda today. Not after the conversation we'd had the day before.

"Love, once the police leave, I think we should send everyone home," Thom said with kind eyes. "I will help you lock up, and all."

"Are you crazy, Thom? I can't send the staff home and still pull off this luncheon!"

"I don't think she's the crazy one," Luke interjected.

"What?"

"Nash, you can't be serious, can you? You can't do the lunch-in thing."

"Luke, shut up. I don't work for you."

His eyes said "Ow." I knew I shouldn't have said that, but I'd had enough of him, and I couldn't afford to lose control of my staff just then.

Thom and Luke just glared at me, like they'd come upon someone peeing on a wall. Fortunately, rescue was around the corner. Literally. Detective Grant Daniels—who had been involved with the team from homicide—came walking from the kitchen to where I was sitting at the counter.

"Pardon me, Gwen. Can I see you a sec?"

"I already gave your guys a statement."

"I know. It's not about that."

"What, then?"

"You have to close it down today," he said.

"Why? You gonna order takeout for the department, make up for my shortfall?"

"No, but I've already told the chief I'm leaving early. We can get away for the afternoon, okay?"

"Okay? I already told your *CSI: Nashville* team I didn't see anything or hear anything. A little sweet talk isn't going to make me remember. Besides, do you not understand? I'm up for Best Mid-Range Restaurant in Nashville! That's important to me. My family never won that. I just need my bread, if it hasn't been marinating in blood, and also for all your people to leave. *That's* what has to happen! What's so hard to understand about that?"

Fine. I was sounding a little crazy. I could hear it with my own two ears. But I had a point. To me, anyway.

"Do you really think anyone's going to come?" Grant asked.

"Are you nuts? You see that crowd outside? They'll come. It'll be the biggest bash they've ever had, rubber-necking to see if we got all the blood and guts."

"That's a big ew," Luke said.

"Put a potato in it," I snapped.

"Nash," Grant cooed, "you really should—"

Just then I swore, loudly and foully. I happened to spot Dani talking to someone at the back door. Someone with a tiny tape recorder. *Please God, please don't let it be the* National.

I bolted from the chair, jogged through the kitchen, pulled Dani inside, saw who was outside, and slammed the door. Except that I forgot about the cinder block. Flushed with anger and embarrassment, I pushed it hard with my foot, heard it shatter as it fell from the platform, *then* slammed the door. I heard a low laugh behind it.

"What's wrong?" Dani asked.

"That was Robert Reid, publisher of the *Nashville National.*"

"Duh. He was asking me a question!"

"Did it occur to you to ask me if it was okay to talk to the press?"

"Actually, it didn't," Dani said. "It's, like, free speech and the Second Amendment."

"That would be the First Amendment," Grant shot back, scooting up behind me and looking at me, his nominal girlfriend. Then he put his arms on my shoulders, turned me toward him, and said, "I'll deal with Reid. Like I told you, I think we all need to pack it up for the day."

His take-charge-ness calmed me. Maybe because it was the most attention he'd paid me since Moses was in diapers.

"Fine. I will go home, Grant. Alone. Thom, will you and Luke lock up, since you all obviously know what's best?"

"Gwen, *dude,* you're being a little harsh—"

"What I said before, Luke. Double down."

Those were my last words before walking out the front door. Then I slammed that door like I had the one in back. As it shut, I heard the CLOSED sign fall to the ground.

I didn't care. Someone else could pick it up. The sea of onlookers parted. Moses was no longer in diapers. But as I walked toward the garage, the magnitude of my having lost it began to hit me.

It's too late to do anything about that, I thought.

I wrote an imaginary Post-it and stuck it on my brain.

Note to self: apologize to everyone in the morning.

Chapter 4

It wasn't the first time, and it probably wouldn't be the last. I'd had my share of walks of shame in the past.

There was the Jim Tyler time. I met him at an art gallery opening during my sophomore year at NYU. I remember hearing him put the security chain on the door after I left that morning, but I don't recall it being latched the night before. That was nice. Then there was the guy who rode me so hard, I had a pillow crease on my face all the next morning. That mark lasted longer than the hoped-for relationship, thank you very much, Mr. Reynolds, damn you. And, of course, there was Phil Silver, who managed to put on his pants and socks to "walk me home" before sitting on the edge of the bed and saying "Are you sure?" after I said, "Really, you don't have to." I ended up marrying that jerk. Or maybe I was the jerk. I was still working on that.

But those walks of shame didn't come close to the one I almost had to take after leaving the deli that Friday morning.

This time I'd found a dead man; "contaminated" a crime scene, as I'd overheard the forensics boys muttering; spoiled an important event; hurt my foot kicking a cinder block; insulted my employees; and smashed my boyfriend's heart like a gefilte fish. And to top it all off, it wasn't until I was out the door that I realized all my keys were on the ring I'd dropped in the bread truck. Grant had asked an officer to recover them. Thom scrubbed them clean and left them on my desk. Luckily, I had a spare house key under my doormat for Grant. At least it *was* for him. *Past tense,* I was thinking. If Mother Teresa had been a lesbian and had dated, not even she would've put up with the bile I spewed. The parking garage had a spare set of car keys in case they had to move me. I'd borrow those.

In short, that was one walk of shame I wasn't taking.

It was strange to be walking through downtown Nashville during a weekday. I'd spent almost a year working so hard, indoors, during those prime daylight hours that I really had never stopped to notice the flowers actually hanging from street fixtures, let alone to smell them, or the tranquility that I thought accompanied only nighttime Nashville, save for the chirping WALK signs on every street corner.

In New York I had never appreciated the little things, either. I would always strive to get from point A to point B in record time, letting no person or thing get in my way. I'd punted away my fair share of inconvenient passing taxis, which was not always advisable in heels. I would cross the street wherever I wanted without waiting for the right-of-way, like I do in Nashville. With drivers illegally on cell phones up there, and me texting and walking into low-hanging branches, like other pedestrians, before I even reached the street, it was a miracle I survived. It really did amaze me, though, that with so much chaos going on all around, New York taxi drivers could still spot a fare's slightly extended arm from blocks away, or catch one that rose a second earlier, and still manage to pull over.

But in Nashville? Nashville's a little different.

I'd started to learn that there was a certain amount of relaxation that accompanied being a Southerner. As wary of folks as I had been bred to be up north, most all of them around here treated you like houseguests, not strangers, and expected to be treated the same way. Oh, there are the selfish cows, like Big Red and her schnorrers. But they're the exceptions, and people are still nice to them. It was a new concept for me, one that took lots of discipline to remind myself of, and even more persuasion to enact.

Even though my dad and his brother Murray had lived here for over twenty years, I had stayed behind in Manhattan and had become an accountant and a wife with a starter marriage. It was not easy for me to shake that New Yorkiness from the blood and reflexes. From what I'd heard about Nashville in the early eighties, it sounded a lot like New York in the early seventies: gritty, seedy, pornographic, and unregulated, with dirty sidewalks, and a magnet for incredible talent. Although I didn't get it at the time, I'm pretty sure all that creative flow pouring out onto the streets made my dad feel really at home here.

Something I'd wished I could've felt myself at that moment.

I was well past the garage and kept walking. I needed to enjoy the sun and shake out the metallic taste in my mouth, a combination of imagined blood and latte, which was all I'd ingested. I didn't feel like going down to busy Broadway, where there was sure to be a dozen cabbies circling for tourists, waiting to take them to one of the few major hot spots they actually knew how to get to. I walked along Harrison instead. While waiting for the light to change on the corner of Tenth, I stood looking down at my pale toes in my spare pair of flip-flops, which I'd put on after the police took custody of my bloody shoes. I guess they wanted to compare them to any other footprints they found. Or didn't find.

As I waited for the light to change, minding my business, a heavily made-up, big-haired lady started toward me from the other end of the block. She was giving me the once-over as she approached. I didn't know her, had no idea what she wanted, and quite frankly was threatened by the beeline she was making toward me.

"Hi. I'm Crystal. From the salon down the block."

"Hi," I said back, certain that she had never done my hair. I went only to Amanda, a transplant from Newark, New Jersey. That was close enough geographically and culturally for us to bond.

"I saw you pass by a minute ago. You have such gorgeous hair. I'd really love to work with it. Here's my card."

"Thanks," I sputtered, tucking it in the back pocket of my jeans, unable to believe that on top of the no-good, very bad day I was having, some scissor jockette would have the nerve to pick on my frazzled brunette hair at a time like this.

"You're the owner of the deli, aren't you?" Crystal asked. "The one they're all talking about?"

"No, I'm Golda Meir," I said.

The woman seemed puzzled. "I thought your name was Katz."

"It is," I said. "Nice to meet you."

I moved on, leaving a confused hairdresser in my wake.

Stopping at the pharmacy on Rosa and Jefferson, I bought the blondest dye-it-yourself gunk I could find and turned back toward the parking garage, taking care not to walk past the hair salon.

The mid-morning drive was quiet, uneventful, and utterly unmemorable. Truly, I didn't remember driving home. I used Grant's ex-key to get inside, and I closed the door, dramatically falling back against it, like someone had been stalking me down an alley. And maybe there had been. I couldn't be sure anymore. I imagined all eyes on me after Crystal hunted me down like a trophy. Maybe they were; maybe they weren't. It felt like it. I told myself, *You're home,* and set the key on the counter. I didn't want any surprise visitors.

It was only a little past eleven a.m., but I was already exhausted. Perhaps from the day's events, perhaps just from walking on my out of shape, former New York legs. I got in the shower, scrubbed my hands like Lady Macbeth, washed my hair, tore open the hair dye, administered the blond treatment, put on the thin plastic hair cap, and sat on the couch with my laptop, checking e-mails and reading the local news, as I waited for Nashville's official hair color to sink in.

The words were a whirlpool in front of my eyes. All I could see was Joe, dead Joe, pieces of Joe, and a lot of bread. They were tesserae of an absurd mosaic of homicide. It wasn't that I hadn't seen dead bodies before. I'd been to open-casket funerals, and I'd seen two people run down in Manhattan, one of them bounced about ten feet high on Central Park West before coming down on the dog he was pulling behind him. Both died. Then there was the guest at Lolo Baker's party who fell through the ceiling into my catered spread a few weeks before.

This was different. Not just because of the blood, but because it had happened at my place.

What had *really* happened? I wondered. It had all started off so well. I was proud that I'd found a compromise with

Brenda. I'd felt like I had a good shot at the prize. It was a photo-album perfect day filled with challenges I knew I could beat like pizza dough. What went wrong? Why did Joe Silvio pick today to become the late Joe Silvio?

Logic hit a wall. That's when imagination takes over to get you through.

Am I next? Was I actually followed home? Am I really a suspect, but I just haven't been subpoenaed? Can that even happen?

What was the press going to do to this? I'd slammed the door on the *Nashville National,* which was one of the sponsors of the competition. Robert Reid had probably been there to cover it.

I had better call them, right? I should prepare a statement or something! Call my lawyer to prepare a statement. I should call him, anyway, in case I was arrested.

Crap. *Crap.*

I told myself to chill. *Let them all come to you. That way, you'll have the energy to deal with this.*

But what if the killer found me first? The police weren't guarding my door. I had even told Grant to stay away—maybe that was the reason he wanted to spend time with me? Bless him, but damn him for not telling me. Hell, what if killing baker Joe was a warning to me?

Warning you of what? Don't be voted Best Mid-Range . . . or else?

I told myself that there was only one thing to do.

Go rinse your hair.

I put my laptop aside and returned to the bathroom. If I was going to lose my mind, my life or, most importantly, the Best in Nashville Award, at least I'd lose it in style. Walking to the sink, I jumped as my cell phone buzzed. I went back to the living room and trolled through my purse until I found it. I didn't recognize the number, although it was local, so I let my voice mail take the call.

I anxiously waited out the minute it took for the voice message icon to appear; then I quickly held the one button for the new message.

"You have one new voice message . . . ," said the robotic voice-mail lady. "New message."

"Hi, Gwen. This is Rob Reid from the *National.* I'm so sorry for all you're going through. I spoke with one of your employees earlier about rescheduling . . ."

Oh. Shit, I thought. *That's what he was asking Dani?*

"And I think we've come up with a workable plan. We want to try and keep the process on schedule. I've talked with the committee and with the editor here, and we're just gonna go ahead and meet at my place Sunday, from seven to nine p.m. It's not exactly a luncheon, then, but it's the next time everyone is free and I've got the room. . . ."

Of course you do. Your daddy owns the newspaper chain.

"What I was hoping, Gwen, was that you could just do a take-out version of whatever you were planning for this afternoon. I know you were kinda stressed this morning, and understandably so, but I was thinking this might help put it behind you. Let me know, okay?"

"To save this message, press nine. To delete this message, press . . ."

I pressed nine.

Well, the good news was that if I went, I wouldn't have to bring food for myself. I'd be eating crow. I knew Robert Reid only by sight, since he was in his own newspaper at least once a week, giving this trophy, cutting that ribbon, giving somebody a prize or a medal or a citation. I shouldn't have assumed he was like every other publisher of every other tabloid I read in the nail salon, out to get a salacious, sensational story.

Not that I'd blame him. *You read those damn papers, don't you? You like peeking into the lives of the rich and powerful. You're glad that their problems aren't your problems, spread across the public consciousness.* Scandal is always entertaining in the third person.

My phone buzzed again.

Thinking it was Robert Reid calling back, I answered.

"Hello?"

"Hey."

It was Grant.

"Oh. Hi."

"Look, I'm sorry to have overruled you in your own place, but you didn't seem yourself. You were a mess, and I thought someone needed to take charge."

"Did you call to make me feel better? 'Cause so far you're sucking at it."

"I called to explain why I stepped on your toes."

"Okay. You explained."

"Gwen, I didn't call to fight."

"If you hadn't called, we wouldn't be." I knew that was harsh, even as it came out of my mouth. The fact that it *had* come from my mouth meant it was in play. Might as well see where the bitch ball landed.

"Is that what this is about?" he asked. "Do you not want me to call anymore?"

I might have hesitated a bit too long on this one, but I wasn't sure. "No," I hedged till I figured it out. "But you hurt me. What you call 'taking charge' I would describe as 'kicking to the curb.' You should've just let me get about my business. They're still having the meeting, you know."

"I heard."

"It would've worked itself out."

"Maybe. Of course, you were the one who stormed off. I was trying to transition things from a crime scene back to neutral."

"Well, I'm not very good at idling."

"I know."

"I make ninety-degree angles. Top speed."

"I know that, too."

"You're a knowledgeable guy," I said. "Now, don't you have a killer to catch?"

"I'm waiting for the autopsy and forensics reports to come back."

"Good. I . . . holy *crap!*"

"What is it?"

"Grant, I . . . *wow! Damn!* I've gotta wash my hair *now!*"

"What?"

I hung up. My scalp was burning up. I'd never gone blond before, but I was pretty sure it wasn't supposed to hurt. I tossed the phone on the couch, next to my laptop, and shuffled my way to the side of my bathtub, turned on the faucet, and knelt beside the tub, removing the skull-cap and purging my head of toxic dye beneath the blessed running water. The initial coolness actually felt really great. I rinsed my hair thoroughly, reached blindly for my hanging towel, and wrapped my aching head in it.

Maybe I should've just taken Crystal's advice and paid for her hair services. And Grant didn't deserve what I had dished out, either, but I couldn't help myself. I'm still that much of a New Yorker: get out of my way, or I'll elbow you.

What I had to learn was that, in the process, I could also do serious damage to my elbows.

Chapter 5

Happily, I went through a scarf phase in college.

I had called Thom and had told her that we would be opening the next day, which she had already guessed, and that we'd regroup and reorganize for a catered affair on Sunday night. She didn't ask me anything of a cautionary nature, like "Are you sure you're up for this?" or "Can you really stand to be around all the committee members and rival restaurateurs?"

Thom was a friend, and she was a pro. She said she'd alert the troops.

I spent the rest of the day losing myself in some TCM movie with Charlton Heston and Eleanor Parker and an army of ants eating up a plantation. Heston won. So did Burt Lancaster in a movie about an Indian raid. I also tried to deal with the bad dye job. I finally gave up and slept a whole four hours that night. Upon waking, I gave in to the reality that I would have to spend the day with a sexy burnt-orange, canary-yellow head, all of it neatly tucked under a strategically placed head scarf. Throw on my finest pair of gold hoops to distract, and voilà! It wouldn't be so bad.

I decided to forgo my Starbucks latte and brew my

own coffee that morning instead of doing my usual stop. I wanted to limit public appearances as much as possible until this whole dead bread guy, crazy hair thing blew over.

Which it would do, right? The thing would die down until they made an arrest.

Or not.

I parked my car as usual in the garage, reluctantly said hello to Randy, and as I rounded the corner of Union on foot, I was greeted by WSMV Channel 4 news setting up their camera equipment. It was too late to turn around and go through the back entrance. I had been spotted by the over-teased, big coral-lipped reporter Candy Sommerton. Sommerton clicked her too-high heels as fast as she could over to me, which looked a little tricky considering the tightness of her skirt and matching blazer, which strained to stay buttoned against her greatest asset. There was a rumor that she had actually been the test model for a 3-D newscast.

"You must be Gwen. I'm—"

"I know who you are, but I really need to get in and open up."

"This will just take a second. Dave, come over here. Let's get a medium shot in front of the Murray's sign. Or better yet, can we set up in the back, where the murder took place?"

Murder.

It sounded so horrible used in a sentence. I guess I hadn't fully committed to the idea that Joe was murdered. Not that I believed his neck spontaneously combusted or anything, though I did feel like that was about to happen to me.

I pushed my way past Lady Longlegs and her goon and reached in my bag to put my key in the front door—the key I forgot that I didn't have. I rapped hard on the glass.

"Gwen, wait!" I heard more heel clicking. I wished I could've clicked mine and just disappeared.

The latch turned, and the door swung open. Thomasina was standing behind it, ushering me in with a protective arm and a body check, like this was Studio 54 in its heyday. The door slammed shut behind me, almost taking the lipstick off Sommerton's mouth.

"Thanks," I said.

I looked around at my full staff. They were relatively relaxed, except for Luke, who had his guard up a little.

"Nash, darlin', you okay?" A.J. half smiled.

"Yeah."

Her twenty-year-old daughter sighed. "Sounds like y'all had quite an adventure. Sorry I didn't start a day earlier."

"I will schedule the next homicide on one of your working days," I told the nearly six-foot-tall Olive Oyl of a young woman.

A.J. Two was not amused. "Y'know, Gwen, I'm a psychology major. We would call what you just did displacement, or *Verschiebung* in German, which means to 'shift' or 'move.'"

"Sorry," I said. "I was just trying to be funny."

"*Try harder!*" said Luke, playing the role of the heckler. He'd heard enough of them to know what they sounded like.

"You need to confront whatever is bothering you head-on," A.J. Two continued.

"I will, later," I said. "All right, group, listen." I ignored the tapping on the front door, did not even turn to scowl at Ms. Sommerton. "I will apologize to you all individually when I have the time. Right now, please accept a big, fat blanket apology so we can get to work. Deal?"

Everyone nodded or repeated the word in the affirmative. Except Dani.

"Are we opening today or just talking?" she asked.

"We're opening," I said. "And we're preparing for a rescheduled catering gig Sunday night."

"Okay, good. Because I went through the bread to make sure there wasn't blood on it, *then* went to the store and bought Wonder Bread, like Thomasina said, to serve people who might be a little sickened by the idea of bread truck bread. I don't want all that work to be wasted."

"It won't be," I assured her.

"She also bought Twinkies," Thom added.

"I thought people might like something cheerful today," Dani said.

I actually liked that idea. "Tell you what. Let's give them away to all the kids."

New Yorkers would've been horrified by the idea of a free mega-sugar fix handed to their precious offspring. Down here that would be considered an act of great hospitality.

"Anybody know how long the reporters have been here?" I asked.

"Since last night," Thom said. "I drove by to make sure the place was okay after they took the tape down. Our outside menus were all ripped off—souvenirs, I'm guessing."

"We'll have to watch that today with our regular menus," I said.

"Right," A.J. the elder said. "Because they're not a hundred years old and shouldn't be replaced, like I've been suggesting."

"Not the time," I pointed out.

"Nash, we're all prepped, so I'm opening shop," Thom said. "I'll tell the press they can't come in and film, but if they want to eat—"

"They'll shoot with cell phones, anyway," Luke said.

"Can't prevent that," Thom said. "I just don't want the bright lights."

"Why not?" Dani asked. "Maybe we can get a tan."

I hoped that was a joke.

Thom went to open the door. I heard her swear. I turned.

Sommerton was interviewing the Repeat Returners. The ones who had heard my argument with the dead man's wife.

"She was *yellin'!*" Blondie exclaimed. "She was sayin', 'I better get my order first thing tomorrow or else' and 'You will be sorry, lady baker woman!'"

Before I could stop myself, I elbowed past Thom and lunged at the camera. Clawing and ripping at the cables and pulling wires, I yanked a long, skinny black cord as hard as I could, ripping the mic from Sommerton's hand. I watched as it flew through the air like half a nunchuck. The cameraman lost his balance and fell backward into the white broadcast van, which pulled a cable that was still in my hand, so that I tumbled forward onto the sidewalk, my head scarf flying off to reveal my fried orangey-yellow hair. A crowd had gathered. Looking up from the ground, I recognized the hairstylist who had approached me just yesterday. She went from horror to manic laughter in about two seconds.

Cell phones were out; pictures and videos were being taken. I hoped some new technology came along soon, because I knew that from that moment forward I would have a posttraumatic reaction to the back side of a cell phone.

Luke and Newt ran to my rescue. Newt strong-armed

the cameraman into quickly packing his gear and leaving. I saw Sommerton give her card to the three ladies as Luke untangled me and picked me up in one swift motion.

"You can expect a bill for the equipment, Ms. Katz!" Sommerton said shrilly.

"Hey, come back when I'm playing on open mic night," Luke said as she turned away.

Without a word I limped into my office, went into my top desk drawer, grabbed an "in case of emergency" cigarette, unlocked the emergency-exit bar, and I stepped quietly, shaken, out the back door. The cinder block was still on the ground, so I stood there with the door propped against my shoulder.

I sucked on my cigarette while staring at the empty concrete in front of me. Just yesterday I had found a dead body out here. It could have been a normal day. I could have been voted Best Mid-Range Restaurant. But no. Someone *had* to do this, and in my backyard.

Nash, someone is dead, my brain reminded me. *Stop obsessing over the Best in Nashville Award!*

Why? I asked. *I want it. For me, for my uncle.*

Fine, but you're losing it.

The award?

Your mind!

I blew smoke. *Touché, brain!*

I stomped out my half-finished cigarette and made my way back in. I needed to dig into some paperwork while my staff did its thing. I also needed to find a new bread company, since I wasn't sure Brenda would want to send one of her trucks back into the kill zone. I also didn't really want to have bread trucked in from Brentwood, as I'd threatened. Perfect excuse to lock myself in my office.

I sat in my old, ratty office chair, which was missing a wheel, replaced instead by a tennis ball. I could have gotten a new one, but it was comforting that my dad had sat in this chair almost every day. What would he or Uncle Murray have done with all this madness?

Keep moving. Keep grooving. And Uncle Murray would most certainly listen to Johnny Cash.

I logged into my Pandora account and typed *Johnny Cash* into the search box. "Folsom Prison Blues" came on. I felt a chill. I really hoped it wasn't a foreshadowing of anything.

One hour and four decades of country classics later, I had locked down a new bread company for right now, and as a courtesy, they were delivering a few bags before the dinner rush. I wished I had known they could do same-day two days ago. Then I wouldn't be in this mess. I reached into my desk drawer for a celebratory Kit Kat as the phone rang.

"Murray's Deli," I said with as much enthusiasm as I could, expecting it to be a reporter.

"Gwen Katz?" said a stern, unfamiliar man's voice.

"Speaking."

"This is Officer Jason McCoy. My brother-in-law Joe Silvio was found dead on your premises yesterday."

"Oh. Sorry for your loss—"

"I understand you were supposed to meet him at your place that morning?"

"Actually, he was supposed to be here and gone by the time I arrived," I said. There was a ball of something forming in my throat, like a hair ball. "Look, I spoke to the police about this yesterday. I don't see what—"

"What you see isn't important," he said. "There's something you need to *understand*. This was a family member. A much-loved family member. He was like a brother to me."

"Understandable. He was your brother-in-law."

"Don't give me sass. I have some questions for you. How well did you know Joe?"

Sass? That was the least of what I wanted to give him. "Officer McCoy, are you on the Nashville PD?"

"Seven years."

"Then you know Detective Daniels?"

"Just answer the question. Either that, or you're going to have a thin blue line that doesn't answer your alarm when it goes off. And it will."

I couldn't believe I was hearing this. We were in Nashville, not New York. And even in New York that kind of thing happened mostly in the Bronx.

"Did you just threaten me, Officer McCoy?"

"How well did you know Joe?"

I decided to see where this was going. "Like I told some not-so-thin members of your blue line, I *didn't* know him. We'd occasionally spoken by phone for business. And he called me that morning, but I wasn't here to take the call. The cops have a recording of that."

"Hey, I don't like the term *cops,*" he snapped. "It's disrespectful. Call us police."

"Call me Ishmael," I said.

"What?"

"Call me a cab."

"Lady, are you crazy?"

"*Call Northside 777,*" I said. "Crazy? I'm getting there." I had to turn this into a game. If I took it seriously, I'd scream till my throat was raw.

"Lady, this may be a joke to you, but my dear sister, Joe's wife, has just lost her beloved husband. Her anchor. Her business partner. Do you understand the pressure that puts on a family? Her husband's dead, and you're making jokes."

"Officer, I understand. You're all in mourning. And frankly, maybe you're not thinking clearly. So perhaps you'd better hang up, take a step back, and tend to your sister. Because from where I sit this is harras—"

"I don't think you *do* understand!" Officer McCoy shouted into the phone like a delayed-reaction firecracker. "What are you not telling us? Where were you Friday morning? Why were you alone with my brother-in-law?"

"I was alone with a corpse!" I screamed. "Are you insane?"

My office door cracked open slightly, and I looked over as a face appeared. Grant! I'd never been so happy to see him.

I put a shush finger to my lips and punched on the speaker.

"I'm sorry, Officer McCoy. Would you repeat the question?"

"I said, 'Why were you alone with my brother-in-law?' I don't believe he was necessarily a corpse, like you say. Not until you made him one! Why?"

"Okay, Officer. I confess. Only not about being with your brother-in-law. I was with Detective Daniels, who happens to be with me. Would you like him to confirm it?"

It was a lie, but it was all I could think of to put this *shmendrick* in his place.

"Why, you slimy New York—"

"Watch that," I cautioned. I knew what was coming next.

Grant jumped in before things got worse. "Jason?" he barked. "What the hell are you doing, man?"

"Talking to your friend."

"I hear that. On whose authority?"

"My own," he said.

"Your own. Where in the regulations is 'your own authority' a reason to interrogate a suspect?"

I stared up at him like I was looking at Bernini's

David in human form, all heroic and stern but with clothes on.

"Detective, I was following up on—"

"A family matter?"

"I thought she might have remembered something—"

"First of all, this is not your case. Second, you can't just call someone and go fishing! She's a victim here, too. You know better, don't you?"

"Ordinarily, but I'm under emotional duress."

That line was a buzzword for internal affairs, in case I pressed charges.

"Then I suggest you stick to supporting your family at this time and stop *trying* to do police work. Clear?"

"Clear, sir."

Grant punched off the speaker, then looked down at me.

"Gwennie, you okay?"

"Your slingshot saved me."

"What?"

"Not important," I said.

Grant's cologne smelled better than ever as I stood and let him hold me. Just for a second. I was on duty, too. No back-room shenanigans.

"Thank you, Grant. Good timing, as usual." I frowned. "Wait, why are you here?"

"Just checking on you," he said.

After the protective rant, that sounded ominously insincere.

"Grant, what is it? Hold on. You said . . . Am I a suspect?"

He hesitated. "No."

"Just no? Not 'No way in hell, Gwennie. What ever, *ever* made you think that stupid, insane thought?'"

"You saw how it is." He dipped his forehead at the

phone. "You're going to feel like one until we wrap this up."

"What about the grieving widow? Maybe she had something to gain, like an insurance payout. I hear a lot of my suppliers aren't doing so good."

"We'll get to her when the time is right," he said. "She's being tranquilized."

"I'll bet, to keep her from spilling her guts," I said. "Maybe hubby dearest had a girlfriend. Maybe he had a boyfriend. Maybe his wife did. Maybe someone was trying to corner the bread market."

"Gwen—"

"Don't! Jesus, Grant, I am a suspect!"

"You're not—"

"What happened to the Bill of Freakin' Rights?"

"Dani got a hold of it," he quipped.

I grinned. It felt good. We needed that tension breaker.

"You're still innocent until proven otherwise," he went on, "but I had a feeling that something like this was going to happen. They're going to rally around Jason, try their best to make you buckle."

"Grant, I didn't do it!"

"I know, but . . . they give everyone a course in the psychology of homicide, and part of it is to keep witnesses in the zone, so to speak. Keep them reliving the crime, the fear, the disorientation. That helps them remember details. Sometimes days later, sometimes weeks."

"Weeks? You're going to let them ride me?"

"I can't be everywhere," Grant said. "That's one of the three reasons I came here. I just got this vibe at the station house. I wanted to let you know that it isn't personal. Not even with Jason."

"That's so not reassuring." I made a face. "What are the other two reasons you came here? Do I even want to know?"

"Well, the second was to see how you are—"

"Skip that one."

"And the third was to tell you good news. The victim had his throat gouged, obviously, and there're traces of canine saliva near the wound."

"Maybe he stopped to pet a dog—"

"It was on the surface of the blood."

"Ah. That explains my sudden urge to sneeze all over the corpse. I'm allergic to them."

"I know. Since you don't have any dogs, we're having to look in different directions for motive and suspect."

I stood upright, like I'd been kicked in the tush by a mule. "Different? You're saying I *was* a suspect!"

"No—"

"Yes! Of course! A guy I've spoken to on the phone is late with my bread, so I'm gonna go all *Vampire Diaries* on his throat. Makes complete sense."

"You're not being fair," Grant said. "You knew all of that, but we didn't. We had to confirm it. That's why it's called an investigation."

I calmed down. He was right. I was just Bathsheba having a very bad day.

"We good?" he asked.

"We're good," I said. "So a dog killed him."

"Well, no."

I looked into his eyes, all strong and steady, while mine suddenly still itched. "What then? A werewolf?"

He smiled. "What I mean is, there are no traces of dog other than what was probably a short series of licks. He died from multiple stab wounds."

"What? And Old Yeller just happened along, drawn by the smell of freshly baked bread and an open jugular?"

"We don't know," Grant said. "We're going over the impounded truck and talking to Metro Animal Care and Control. Still putting it all together."

"What about that rye bread up front?" I asked as the whole vignette came back in an ugly flash.

"Probably got knocked forward. They were on the bottom shelf."

"So the killer came in through the back?"

"Or left that way. Or it was the dog. Or the truck was shaking hard from a struggle. We just don't know yet."

"But you've ruled out it being a message."

"What kind of message?"

"You know, like 'Joe sleeps with the genetically engineered grains.'"

"We don't think so," he replied.

I took a moment to digest it all. That was sure one hell of a roller-coaster five minutes. Thinking of digestion made me realize how hungry I was.

"I'm going to get something to eat," I said. "Want something?"

"Sure," he said.

"Wait here. I'll bring it back."

I left the office to quickly throw together a simple spread, but I couldn't bring myself to eat anything more than some leftover matzo ball soup. I don't know if it was nerves or just the image of raw human meat branded in my brain.

Grant's cell went off midway through his pastrami on a sun-dried tomato wrap. It was the precinct. I stood to get him a to-go box.

"Anything?" I asked when I returned.

"A domestic squabble," he said. "At Jason's house."

Sweet Baby James. "I'm sorry," I said, and I meant it.

"How about some Chinese and a Blu-ray tonight?" he asked as I walked him to the door.

"Danny boy, I don't want to sound ungrateful, but I just kinda want to be alone."

He shrugged off a little bit of hurt. "Whatever you need."

"I appreciate it, Grant."

"Including some Clairol. I'm not certain orange is your color."

"Long story."

"I'm just looking out for you," he said. "Someone might mistake you for Rita Hayworth's daughter."

If we hadn't been in the dining room, I'd've kissed him. He knew it. He winked. I smiled. He left.

I needed a quick break, a moment to get my feet under me again. I turned to Old Reliable, who was making change.

"Thom, I'll be back before the early dinner rush. We okay with the catering?"

"If we're not, butts will be torched."

I went back to the office, got my bag, and set out, ignoring the eyes on me, the thought bubbles I could practically read above the heads of my customers. I *was* a suspect; I *wasn't* a suspect; Cujo was to blame. I'd had enough. It was definitely time to take my life back. I just needed to meet with someone head-on, face-to-face. To clear my account with them and restore my good name.

I started walking, suddenly aware that my calf muscles were sore. Of course they were. I hadn't really walked on pavement for a lot of blocks for nearly a year. As I picked my way through another sunshiny day, I called 411. I still hadn't learned how to work my phone's GPS. And though I didn't have the heart to tell Grant, my eyes couldn't tell the difference between a Blu-ray disc and a VHS tape. The heartbreak of being a Luddite.

"Four-one-one. City and state, please," the female operator said.

"Nashville, Tennessee," I responded.

"What listing?"

"McCoy's Bakery," I answered, over-pronouncing the words. "I believe it's somewhere off of Demonbreun Street."

That's what comes from online bill paying. No envelopes, no writing an address, no idea where you're going.

"One moment please."

"Listen, I just want the—"

Too late. The operator switched to the automated phone number provider before I had a chance to request just the address.

"The number you are looking for is, area code six-one-five-five-five-five-six-two-oh-three. To dial directly for an additional charge, press one, or just stay on the line."

I could barely remember what day it was—Saturday, I realized from the number of families on the street who were not churchgoers, which would have made it Sunday. I could barely remember *that,* let alone a phone number. I sucked it up and accepted the charge. I just needed to know where I was headed. After two rings, someone answered.

"McCoy's Bakery, where all your *kneads* are met. This is Eric."

"Hi ya, Eric." I put on my best random customer voice. "I was just wondering where exactly you're located."

"We're in downtown Nashville, ma'am."

"Yes. Where exactly, though?"

"Between the dry cleaners and Enslin's Auto Parts."

"Okay, Eric," I said, my character starting to fade. "I'm looking for the street address."

"We're at three-oh-four Sixth Avenue South."

"Thank you very much," I said and hung up. And realized that my name had probably appeared on their caller ID gadget thing. Hopefully, the little LED letters would evaporate before anyone with Brain One could see them and remember who I was.

I continued walking south the few additional blocks toward Sixth South. There was a slight breeze. It felt sweet. Few things had in the last thirty-six hours.

Except Heston and those miles of flesh-eating ants, I thought. His tsuris seemed a little worse than mine.

"Three-oh-four, three-oh-four," I kept repeating as I neared Sixth.

And suddenly there it was, McCoy's Bakery, a one-story brick building sandwiched between greasy car parts and clean sheets. There was something unsettling about the weird juxtaposition. It was like bad geometry, lines that didn't match. Was the universe trying to tell me something, like this was probably a bad idea?

"Do what needs doin'," I said, repeating one of Thom's frequent admonitions under my breath.

As I reached for the door handle, I pulled when I should have pushed. That was my last warning, apparently. I pushed and entered.

Several customers were being helped one at a time by the sole employee, who was calling numbers on those little machine-dispensed slips of paper. I reached for my number and pulled the paper from the red plastic spool.

I was number forty-nine. The glowing number counter on the wall said forty-five.

Since I wasn't there to buy bread, I wasn't sure I needed a number, but I decided to wait my turn. That way I would have the employee's full attention and would not annoy, too much, whoever had the next number.

As I watched the tall, red-haired kid behind the counter slowly assist each customer, I was reminded of a bakery joke my uncle used to tell:

An alien lands on Earth, walks into a bakery, and

asks the owner, "Excuse me, earthling. What are these miniature wheels for?"

"Oh, they're not wheels," the baker responds. "They're bagels."

Confused, the alien purchases one and takes a bite. The alien's eyes grow wide. "Wow!" he says to the baker. "These would go great with cream cheese and lox!"

Uncle Murray was a card. But it was an ace. Thinking of Officer McCoy made me miss my own support circle, of which Murray was a big part, especially after my folks died.

"Number forty-nine? Forty-nine?"

"Here!" I made my way to the display case filled with pastries and rolls.

"How can I help you?"

"Brenda's not in today, is she?"

"Negative. She's dealing with some personal stuff."

"May I speak with a manager?"

"We don't have one, really. I mean, you may have heard what happened?"

"Yes, I'm sorry."

"Yeah, so it's just me and Eric today, and he's back there baking right now."

"You gonna order?" someone behind me asked.

"Give me a bagel with schmear," I said.

"With what?"

"Cream cheese."

"What kind of bagel?"

"Raisin."

"We only have plain and onion."

Of course you do. "Plain," I said.

"How is Brenda taking all this?" I asked.

"Bad," he said as he sliced the bagel.

"Understandable. It happened during a delivery?"

"Yeah."

"At a deli, I heard."

"Yeah."

"Who do you think is responsible?"

The kid finished spreading a thin, gentile layer of cream cheese and started wrapping the bagel in tinfoil—not wax paper. "I don't know," he said.

"What does Brenda think?"

"That'll be a dollar fifty," he said.

I gave him a credit card to buy some time. I heard a groan from the small group behind me.

"I don't know what she thinks," the boy said as he waited for the receipt to print. "All I know is I went looking for the meat cleaver yesterday to divvy the dough and it was gone. I mentioned it to her, and she said not to worry about it."

"Really? Where do you think it went?"

He put the receipt on the counter with a pen. He was looking at me a little funny.

"I think she took it for protection," he said. "I think she's nervous."

"Lady, you're gonna need protection if you don't sign the goddamn bill!" someone shouted.

So much for kind and patient Nashvillians. I signed.

"Say, do I know you?" the kid asked suddenly.

"No," I replied.

"Yes," he disagreed. "I saw you on TV this morning."

"That isn't exactly knowing—"

"You were on the news."

"Hey, you watch TV?" I said. "I was under the impression kids watched everything on their cell phones."

"It was on in the back room," he said. "Yeah, you were on with Candy Sommerton."

"No," I said. Truth was, I was *on* Candy Sommerton. I turned to find myself blocked in by five cross-looking patrons. I started to push my way through.

"Yes," the boy said. "You were on the sidewalk. She was yelling at you!"

"That was some other deli owner," I said, then swore. I was nearly at the door, but I had forgotten my bagel. It wasn't that I needed it or even wanted it; I had to have it. Just to make a statement that no mob was going to push me around. I started digging my way back. Old Man Number Fifty was asking to be served *now*. He scowled at me as I thrust an arm in front of him to grab the paper bag. I glowered right back.

You don't mess with a New Yorker. And that's what I was, wherever I happened to be living.

As I walked back toward Murray's, I stopped at a convenience store and bought myself a fresh pack of Natural American Spirits. I tore the cellophane off, pulled one out, and lit a match.

Glowering? Walking the streets? Smoking? Was I secretly despising the transplant I'd become? Was I trying to destroy myself in an unhealthy, angry blast of blaming it on the dead deliveryman? And then the dreadful thought occurred to me.

I really miss who I used to be.

Maybe it was the stress talking, but I had to fight tears as I ignored the disapproving faces and waving hands of everyone who caught a cloud of my smoke.

Chapter 6

Okay, I was officially having an identity crisis.

There was no denying it. I was the one who stood out down here. The one who didn't have a Southern accent. The one person who'd been to the Met and Carnegie Hall but not to the Grand Ole Opry. I was allowed to live here, to give orders to Thom, because my father and uncle were on the inside.

I looked down at the clutter on my office desk, specifically at the crinkled color photo I'd found stuffed in the back of my top desk drawer when I first arrived. It was of my uncle Murray, comfortable in his element, with a guitar in his hands, a smoke dangling from his lips, and another behind his ear, and he was staring right at the camera, at the picture taker. The flashbulb reflected off the sweaty sheen on his forehead and the lenses of his glasses. A couple of girls were glancing sidelong, curious but otherwise disinterested in the wannabe songster sitting at a table in the apparently sleazy nightclub.

Despite terrible audience reviews and very little interest from the industry, at least Murray had spent his free time doing what he really wanted to. Just being himself before he had to get practical and earn money. And here I was, taking a hard look at myself, and all I could think of was that I really should get a frame for the photo, instead of having it pinned to a corkboard with a pushpin. Was that the extent of my desires?

And then there was Detective Grant Daniels. He'd given me all the love and attention one could hope for from a full-time detective. He just wasn't giving me what I really needed, what I really craved, what most divorced women in their thirties wanted: a second chance at an exciting life that was shared, not catch as catch can. I had spent my first marriage worrying about pleasing a man. Now I wanted someone to pay attention to me, to satisfy me emotionally.

Was *that* it? Was that my goal in life?

I didn't know. *Dammit, I didn't know!*

The only thing that had satisfied me in the past couple of months was figuring out who killed a local slimeball and nearly getting myself offed in the process. Was it the thrill or a secret death wish that had made it so exciting?

I didn't know that, either. I wasn't sure I wanted to.

Saturdays at Murray's were always more interesting because most interesting people work during the weekdays, and it was usually lively and interesting when they came out of hiding on weekends. They truly appreciated the time off. I took some bites of bagel and sat back in my chair for one last moment of external peace before returning to the need to make a living.

After fixing my scarf around my fried-egg head, I opened my office door.

The dining room was moderately busy, and Dani and A.J. were picking up orders from under the heat lamp. I sensed animosity between the two servers.

"How we doing?" I asked.

"Stupidly," said Dani.

I wasn't sure what she meant, exactly, but I went with it. "What do you mean?"

"I was talking to my coworker about kosher," Dani said, taking pains to pronounce the word correctly. "I was sayin' how I agreed with y'all because I hated seein' animals killed for eatin'. She told me I was crazy."

"Kosher animals are bled out," A.J. said. "Slowly."

"That's sort of a misconception," I said. "They use a very sharp knife and the killing part happens quickly."

Dani looked a little ill. I didn't feel so great myself; what I had just said made me think of the bread guy in his truck.

"Well, fast killin' or slow, I told her it's the food chain," A.J. continued. "This snot nose never heard of that."

"We don't need name-calling," I said.

"It's okay," Dani told me. "I called her something worse first."

A.J. made a parting face, grabbed her order, and left. Dani took more time gathering her plates and balancing them. She seemed to have a knack for that, at least.

"I'm sorry," she said as she worked, "but I just *hate* it when creatures suffer. I don't mean, like, snakes and flies and lobsters, but cute ones. It really does break my heart."

The sadness in her voice, in her eyes, made me feel like I was watching a young girl say a permanent good-bye to her imaginary friends.

"You know," I said, "maybe you should rethink the fact that you're working in a deli. We do slice and serve a lot of meat here."

"I want to work here," Dani said. "I'm here for a purpose."

"You mean . . . what, exactly? Like God's purpose? Is

it part of a plan?" I wondered if I should make sure all our meat cleavers were secure.

"I really have to serve these meals," she said. "But I think maybe one reason I'm here is to make sure there's more tofu on the menu so we don't have to corn so much beef."

"I see." I did, too. "Tell you what. Do some brainstorming. Come up with a few vegan dishes for the deli."

Dani's eyes lost their sadness as she turned to go. "For real?"

"As real as wheat gluten duck," I replied.

"Thanks, Nash. You won't be sorry!"

"And don't forget open mic night!" Luke shouted from the kitchen. "We need that, too!"

I was heading toward the deli entrance to help Thom bus the tables when I noticed an out-of-place older woman across the street. You couldn't miss her. She was wearing a large black hat with a brim that covered half her face, sunglasses that covered most of the other half, and a tight, formfitting black dress, black tights, and black heels. At first I thought she was squinting to read our deli hours painted on the front door, but her phantom gaze seemed to fall directly on me as I moved throughout the deli. Trancelike, transfixed, as if she were a black widow spider, I opened the front door to see who it was. But when I stepped outside, a brief flare of sunlight on the glass speared my eyes; when it cleared, the woman had vanished.

"Somethin' wrong?"

It was Thom, at my ear.

"No," I said. "I thought . . . I saw someone."

"You thought you saw someone?"

"I thought I saw someone who was looking at me," I

said, making a hash of my attempt to clarify the situation. "Never mind."

"Boss lady, I really think you need to take some time off. And I don't mean just a stroll down the block. I mean some *time*."

"Yeah, maybe," I agreed. "After the Best in Nashville thing."

"You don't need to be there," Thom said. "Brown-nosing the committee isn't going to help. Everyone will be doing it."

"I know. But I have to keep busy. Otherwise, my brain goes *bang*, back to the bread truck."

Thom shook her head. "You gotta learn to think happy thoughts."

"I'm a New York Jewish woman," I said.

"So?"

"If you knew more of us, you'd understand what a challenge you just presented."

Thom shook her head again.

"Tell you what, though," I said. "I'm gonna take a drive. I'm not sure if I'll be back before closing. You got things?"

"A drive where?" she demanded.

"Just out," I lied.

"You're lying."

"I know," I said.

The head shaking evolved into a shoulder-shrugging sigh. "Don't worry about anything here. I'll keep Goofus and Gallant from killing each other."

I kissed Thom on the ear, embarrassing us both. I got my purse, made sure I had my keys, and headed for the door.

"Nash, wait!"

Dani came almost skipping from behind the counter. "I forgot to tell you something."

"What?" My bowels tightened.

"I made a Facebook page for Murray's Deli last night!"

"Wonderful."

"It is!" she said, wigwagging her cell phone. "We've got two hundred forty friends already! I just checked! That's two hundred twenty-one more than the I-Heart-Kosher page I started the day before."

I smiled. That was just wonderful.

I was still smiling stupidly as I left.

Chapter 7

I was headed to Hendersonville, which was more exquisite than a fresh box of chocolates on a lonely Valentine's Day.

Only about twenty minutes from downtown, each sprawling house was more stunning than the last. I snaked through the curves of the exclusive neighborhood, craning and dipping my head to take in the view of each rural palace as I rolled by. I was overwhelmed by the mansions, the giant trees, and the smaller ornamental flowering cherries, trident maples, and redbuds. There were also fountains, dogs running loose in unfenced yards, driveways as long as runways, ponds, lakes, and four-car garages. No wonder country music stars chose to live in this lofty yet reclusive enclave.

As did the *Nashville National's* Robert Reid.

When I rolled up to the Dale Avenue estate—I'd gotten the address from the work order for Sunday's bash—I started to wish I'd called ahead. There were a number of cars in the driveway. His or guests'?

What the hell, I thought. If I didn't get any alone time to apologize for snapping at him the day before, I could always say I was here to check the venue before the event.

Robert's house was a three-story, Tudor-looking mansion, the kind where you could see the timbering-wood beams from the outside and every part of the residence had a giant thatched triangle roof feel to it. Overhanging floors, pillared porches, and a spiraling brick chimney sticking out of every wing. Lush foliage clung to the exterior, and flower gardens lined the stone path leading up to the brick-embossed, stained-glass entrance, which was big enough to comfortably accommodate a giant.

I didn't dare pull in the driveway. That would leave me no quick exit, as if the driveway were the tongue of this massive beast that would never let me escape should I lose my nerve. I parked my car along the street and started the long walk to his front door. The sun filtered through the surrounding trees, bright, dark, bright, dark, like an old nickelodeon slowly turning. The whole thing was like a dream. The killing, my being here, my being divorced, my dad and uncle gone, me being alone.

Stop that! I yelled inside.

A few stone steps away from where I was, the real house steps began, winding up like the grand staircase of Tara. It was all light now, no shade, no darkness.

"Gwen!"

I froze.

"Gwen?"

I looked around—left, right, behind. Of course, the speaker was standing in front of me, at the open door of the mansion. It was Robert Reid.

"Hi!" I said.

"Hi. Security camera saw you. Did I forget that you were coming?"

"Nope," I replied. "I, uh . . . I just thought I'd check the place out before tomorrow. Get the lay of the land."

"Aha." Robert was still a little bewildered but congenial. He was wearing a baby blue, lightweight V-neck sweater, his sleeves partially pushed up, and khakis, with no shoes or socks on. His moderately tan skin accented his short, slick golden brown hair.

"Actually, that isn't entirely true," I said.

"Oh?"

"No." I was still standing at the foot of the steps, talking loud enough for the gardener across the street to hear. I started forward. "No. I really felt I should apologize face-to-face for slamming the door on you. So here I am!"

He stepped onto his front landing, crossed his arms, and leaned his back on the door frame as I struggled to make my way to the top. His golden smile allowed a sweet, forgiving chuckle. He was kind of handsome and pretty well built, now that I took time to notice.

"Here you are," he said. "Can I tell you something?"

"It's your house." I wasn't even sure what that meant. I wanted him to say something fast to wash it from my ears.

"I thought it was kind of funny," he said.

"What was?"

"The look on your face when you tried to close the door on the cinder block."

I felt myself flush.

"I was half betting myself that you would actually succeed in pulling the door *through* it."

"Hulk smash," I said. "I wasn't myself."

"Are you now?"

"Much more so," I lied. This was not the time and place to tell him that I was having an identity crisis. I reached the landing. "I've never really been to this side of town. You've got quite a home."

"Thanks. I inherited it from my grandmother."

"Gay," I said.

"That's right."

"She was the one who founded the newspaper chain," I said.

"Right again. After my grandfather died. The family owned a lot of property down here. She started selling it during the boom, bought a bunch of small papers and built them up."

"Quite a woman," I said.

"Most women are," he said.

"How do you mean?" I hoped he wasn't being patronizing. I could use some "sincere" right now.

"Men just have to deal with their own egos. You gals have to deal with men *and* your own identities and ambitions. That's a lot of work."

"Sometimes," I admitted.

He was looking at me funny. I couldn't decide whether it was kindness or pity or whether he was mentally replaying my attack on a concrete mass.

"Well, I'm glad you were home. I hope I didn't interrupt anything."

"No," he said. "I was just on the phone with the office."

"So . . . what's your job there?"

"Apart from being on the board and running things day to day as publisher of the *National*?"

"Yeah, apart from that."

"Nothing."

"Right. I guess those things would keep you kind of busy."

"They do," he said. "Which is why it was also a little amusing that you thought I was interviewing your employee. I haven't done that for years, since my dad brought me on to learn the ropes."

"Like I said, my brain was in lockdown."

"Understandable," he said. "For the record, the *National* decided not to play the story big again until the police have a better idea of what actually happened."

"That's . . . journalistic of you."

"It's a little more self-serving than a case of integrity," he said. "We don't feel sensationalism is good for our city. We are about quality of life and the arts. Murders aren't a good fit."

Well, he was honest, I had to admit

"So, now that I've got that off my chest, I really should get going—"

"I thought you wanted to check the room where the gathering will be held?"

"Right," I said. But I hesitated.

"Let me guess," he said. "You're afraid that will be an imposition? Am I hot or cold?"

"You're hot," I said. "Definitely hot."

"Well, it's not a bit," he replied. "It'll be a pleasure."

Ushered in by his extended arm, I took a walk through the place with him. It was like touring a museum, a small one, devoted to the Reid family. I don't say that in a bad way. There was nothing narcissistic about it. He came from a proud family, and they were rightfully on display here. He wasn't arrogant about it, either. He seemed truly, refreshingly humble to be a part of it.

I shuffled beside him on my sore calves as we crossed the cavernous foyer. It was decorated with massive works of art and ancient-looking tapestries and weapons. I looked up.

"Nice chandelier."

"Thanks. My grandfather had it imported from Paris after his honeymoon stay with my grandmother at the Hotel Regina. He arranged for it to be removed from their wedding night suite. He wanted every night to be their wedding night."

"I guess anything's possible when you're in love."

"For the right price." He grinned. "Come this way."

Robert guided me from the foyer through a small series of hallways that led to the kitchen. My nose tickled, probably from the good dusting this place must get every day. I ignored it as I took in the afternoon sun, which filled the room with calming white warmth that reflected off the gray granite countertops.

"It's a lovely space. I can imagine throwing quite a party in here."

"Yes. I prefer the natural lighting in this room. I rarely turn the lights on during the day."

Keep those electric bills low, I thought. That was a little bitchy, I admit. I used to feel that way when I was handling Godzilla-size accounts on Wall Street, that it would be nice not to have to watch every dollar you spent.

"You live alone?" I asked. The girl-brain part of me was anxious about his reply.

"It's just me and Nancy," he said.

"And that would be Mrs. Reid?"

He smiled. "My Nancy is a rottweiler."

I assumed he meant that as a noun and not an adjective.

"Where is she?" I asked.

"Out back. Naturally, she's high energy, so I fenced in the backyard for her to run around in. If I let her run free, she'd do nothing but birth puppies."

"That'd be a strange life," I said.

"Very."

"Oh," I replied. That would explain the tickling. I had a flash—a horrible gut burn of a moment—that took me back to the delivery truck, back to Robert being out there the next morning, back to my office and hearing

Grant tell me about a canine, then back here. It was like a trip through the Stargate. I told myself the dog situation was unrelated.

Robert moved to the stovetop, where a fresh batch of pastries was cooling.

"Chocolate chip meringues," he said.

"You have an on-premise dessert chef?"

He replied with a half smile that said, "I made them myself."

I was impressed—after feeling stupid, yet again, for assuming that he was just a helpless, spoiled rich kid.

"Yum," I said dumbly.

Robert used the spatula to dislodge the off-white egg-white cookies from the pan and placed them on a nearby serving dish before presenting them to me.

"These look great!" I gushed. "And they smell wonderful. I should hire you to supply the shop on a regular basis. Business would boom."

"Try them first."

And he was modest. He was too good to be true. That was also girl brain. *Beware of men. They lie to get in your jeans. Don't imagine that he's any different.*

I bit into the lightweight dessert and a warm chocolate chip melted onto the cradle of my lip as the thin cookie exterior crunched, then softened as it touched my tongue.

"Robert."

"Yes?"

I just looked at him as I chewed, my closed mouth forming an involuntary smile, my pinkie lightly swiping the chocolate from my lip as I laughed self-consciously. My other arm and my lower back rested against the glistening counter, my right foot and calf flexed backward like during a first kiss.

"Nothing," I said.

"A lot of nothing adds up to something," he replied.

That made a kind of crooked sense. There was that wrong geometry again. That was how everything had been these past few days—everything real but off.

Robert set the serving dish down and closed the distance between us, staring into my eyes as if looking into my confused brain, searching for something without artifice or deflection. He found it—I could tell from his eyes—in the slightly open set of my lips. He gripped me around my waist, tilted his head forward, and pressed his mouth against my left cheek. I held on to the counter for fear that I would float away, even though he had me pinned there. I felt the meringue begin to soften and melt in my hand. My thumb went through it with a crumbling sound. I let the cookie pieces fall rather than interrupt the kiss.

He finally pulled away.

My brain said, *Wow*. So did his eyes. And that was just a cheek kiss.

"I'm sorry," I said, "but is it okay if I put the cookie on the counter?"

He laughed. Which made me laugh.

"You can do whatever you want with it," he said.

"Really?" I smiled and shoved it in my mouth, chomping noisily.

He laughed at my antics. And that was what they were: me being nervous. My fighting a little bit of guilt about Grant. Me not caring, then, about anything but the moment. Another circle through the past to get to the present.

I chuckled at my own predictable behavior.

"What?" he asked with a smile.

"Nothing. Nothing at all."

"Newspaperman, remember?" he said. "I'm good at reading people."

"Profiler!" I said accusingly as I swallowed meringue.

"Guilty," he replied.

"I really am enjoying all this. Really."

"I know. I'm reading that, too."

"Surprising, though."

"Which part?" He laughed.

"The cookies, yeah, but mostly this," I said.

"Yeah," he agreed. "You looked like you could use some grounding. I hope this worked. Even if it *was* a surprise."

"Big-time. But not finding-a-dead body surprising," I said stupidly. Mood killingly. But in my defense, the homicide was kind of a big thing, and it was still lodged firmly in my frontal lobes.

Robert pursed his lips knowingly. He removed my arm from around his neck—how did that get there?—and followed the length of my arm with his hand, down to my wrist. He clutched my hand with his thumb nestled in my palm, his fingers wrapped around the back of my hand.

"You've been through a lot," he said.

"I guess everyone gets a turn at bat."

"What do you mean?"

"Big things. Traumas. I'm sure you've had some."

"Not many," he said, knocking the granite behind me. "When, *if,* I do, though, I hope I'll know where to find you."

That was sudden, also unexpected, somehow more forward than the kiss, and definitely weird.

Robert flashed that ten-million-dollar-house smile, squeezed the hand he still held, broke free from our rapture, grabbed one of his small homemade meringues, and popped the whole thing in his mouth.

"Not bad." He grinned, chomping as I had.

I took a deep breath and suddenly became aware of

my legs again. We started toward our original destination, the dining room. It was down a short hallway from the kitchen and was larger than my home. There was a little too much Louis XVI, silver, and Matisse on the walls for my taste. Well, not the Matisse. There were also deer heads. I made a mental note to limit Dani to kitchen duty.

I looked around, nodding, trying to focus on the room and not the guy in the V-neck.

"Great," I said.

"You approve?"

"You could have a committee meeting or sign a treaty in here," I said. "Yeah, it works."

"Perfect," he said. "You know there's Shakespeare in the Park next Thursday night right outside the Parthenon. Maybe I'll ask you to go to that."

"I've been to the Parthenon only once, but as I recall, it's as close to seeing the real thing in Nashville as I'll get."

"I think that was a compliment to our fair city."

"Probably," I said vaguely.

Robert laughed and kissed me one more time before leading me back through the short maze of hallways and into the foyer. I thanked him again for everything and swayed my way down his footpath, all giddy and self-conscious.

I paused at the car, saw he was still at the door, and waved good-bye before getting in. Robert waved back, his forearms looking manlier than before, then turned and closed his door.

I closed my door. I just sat there.

Oh. My. Good. God.

I sat in my silent car, hunched over and staring fuzzily at the dashboard. I saw my fortune-teller hair poking ugly and raw from my disheveled scarf. He saw that and kissed me, anyway. What a prince.

Start the car and drive away before he looks out and sees you're still sitting here.

I started the car and drove away.

Thinking, unfortunately, not about Robert or about Grant.

What came into my head as I left Hendersonville was that goddamn rottweiler.

As I drove back along the busy highway, I managed to get the dog and the canine traces from the crime scene out of my head by thinking about Grant. I was angry at him, but I wasn't sure why. Probably because he wanted to be around me more than I wanted to be around him. What had just happened with Robert proved that— not just that I was receptive to the kiss but that I really enjoyed it.

I'd made up my mind to sever things with Grant instead of going for the slow-death route. As I got off the highway, I pulled over and felt my jacket pockets for my cell phone.

What the hell?

It wasn't there or in my purse or on the passenger seat or on the floor. Did I leave it at Robert's place? I didn't think so. I hadn't used it since before that. When? I couldn't remember. Most people who wanted to reach me called at the deli. Had I taken it out at the bakery when I went to pay, left it on the counter? After all, I'd forgotten the bagel.

Maybe I'd left it in the office. I had to. Where else could it be?

As my mother used to say, "If your head wasn't screwed on . . ."

Business was busier than usual as I entered the deli. Many eyes were on me, the homicide hag freak with the burned-out hair.

Raylene and A.J. Two were glaring at me from behind

their otherwise customer-attentive eyes. I guess they could've used me instead of Dani today.

Dani got to me first on her way back to the kitchen. She looked perplexed, which was not unusual. "Nash, I think you should know—"

"Not now, Dani," I said as I squirmed my way to the safety of my office.

"But, but," she sputtered.

I kept walking. Now, you're probably thinking, *You should listen to her. She may have something important to say.* The truth is, she had done that to me a lot in the past couple of days. This was no different. It was about the quantum jump in our Facebook "likes" or "friends," or whatever the hell they were. We were up to 873. She had said that was "manly," though she pronounced it *mainly,* so I wasn't sure if she meant it was strong or if *mainly* was a new social networking term that I'd not yet heard, as in mainline-y. It didn't matter. I found it ghoulish.

I put my purse on my desk, slammed the door shut, sat back in my dad's chair, and pulled my scarf from my head. I'd fixed it in the car. My scalp had started to feel cramped.

I looked around my desk, shuffled papers and junk mail here and there, and I didn't see my phone. I even looked under the desk and under my *tuckus,* in case I was sitting on it.

Anxious to get it over with, I picked up the office phone and began dialing Grant's number. But something made me stop. I decided to check my cell voice mail first. Maybe Robert had called and left a message that would spur on the renewed confidence I might need to carry me through the breakup process.

"You have two new voice messages," it said. "First message."

"Hello, Ms. Katz," the stranger's voice said. "This is

Dave Clifton calling with the Nashville Haunted Tour Experience. I was hoping to discuss the possibility of formally adding your back loading area to the experience, as patrons are beginning to request it. We're big fans and would be grateful if you'd call—"

I tapped a button. Part of my brain thought, *That will bring in new clientele, more tourists.* The sensible part of my brain slapped that part down.

"Message deleted. Next message."

"Hi, Gwen."

It was Grant.

"I just want you to know how much I care about you," he said in a monotone, which I didn't think he intended to be ironic. "I really do. You know that. But this just isn't working out. Something's different between us, something has changed, and I just don't think you're interested in finding out what so we can work on it. I tried calling you a couple of times this afternoon to talk it over, but you just aren't calling me back, so I'm guessing it's too late. I even went to get my stuff from your place, but I see the key is already gone. So, yeah. Here it is, my sad good-bye. I'll just collect my stuff when it's convenient, and I'll try not to be too intrusive if I have to talk to you about the case. Be good. And good luck."

He jostled the phone for a second before hanging up.

"End of new messages."

Chapter 8

I sat on my couch, staring at my laptop next to my sleeping cats, surrounded by the things that brought me the most comfort in life. I had just finished washing my hair, rinsing and repeating several times, scrupulously trying to make the color fade, but I'd made very little headway. I wasn't particularly tired, and it was early on a Saturday night, so I drained my glass of pinot grigio and I set it back down on the coffee table. It hit with a hard *cling*. I was apparently a little more impaired than I'd thought.

It was times like these that I couldn't stand being without my cell phone. I picked up Robert Reid's card, which I remembered him having given to me when the chamber of commerce welcomed me to town. I had scoured my home earlier that evening and had found it at the bottom of my kitchen junk drawer, where I put all kinds of business cards and take-out menus, the surviving paper detritus of the modern age.

I was touching the gold embossed lettering of his name when I happened to notice there was an e-mail address on the bottom. It was his name @nashville_national.com, but if he was anything like me, he checked his business in-box more often than his personal one. And I was pretty sure he hadn't called yet to set up that Shakespeare in the

Park date, but I hadn't recently checked my voice mail, so I couldn't be totally positive. Obviously, he was weighing heavily on my mind. I sort of wished he were here right now, though I wasn't sure if it was because I liked him or was in need of his pleasant distraction. Then I got jealous, thinking it was a Saturday night and he must be out with some hot society shiksa.

I decided to shoot him a quick, harmless little, wine-goaded e-mail. I'd simply ask if he had happened to find my phone, even though I doubted I'd left it there. But it would get the point across that I was phonally restricted. If I were interested in someone, I'd want to know that.

I settled my laptop on my legs, which were comfortably stretched on the coffee table, where I happened to get the best Wi-Fi reception.

Subject: Hey old friend

That was ridiculous.

Subject: Quiet Saturday night

That was desperate.

Subject: Did you happen to find my phone? If so e-mail me.

Too long. And impersonal.

Subject: Phone

That worked. I went on.

Hey!
Just wondering if you came across my cell.
Can't find it!
Hope you had a great day.
Gwen
P.S. Any plans tonight?

I hit SEND before I had a chance to think about what my fingers had written without me. As I refilled my glass, I realized that since it *was* Saturday, maybe he wouldn't check his work e-mail until Monday. I suddenly felt foolish and wished I could un-send it.

I took a sip of wine, then filled the cats' bowls so they wouldn't wake me in the middle of the night. I heard a "you've got mail" ping. I hurried back, and the world seemed very warm and sweet and fragrant. It was from Robert!

Re: Phone
Hey, pretty lady!
Negative on the phone. I don't know how you can stand it!
I would be lost without mine.
Want to meet up? Lady's choice.
RR

RR? Rrrrrr, I thought.

I felt like I was sixteen years old again. I took another swig of wine and sat staring at my screen, my face flush from his invite. My fingers were raised on the keyboard like I was about to begin playing Chopin, not scales. What did I want to do?

Hell, I knew what I wanted to do, and I did it.

Re: Re: Phone
Sounds good! Maybe food?
G

It took a whole thirty seconds for him to respond.

Re: Re: Re: Phone
Great! I know a fantastic deli. J/k.
Meet me downtown at Fourth and Broadway in an hour.
RR

Bingo. And yet the girl-brain part of me that wasn't rational wondered why he didn't offer to pick me up. I wondered if I would ever be satisfied with anything.

I slid into a trendy pair of dark jeans, slipped on a tank, layered a few necklaces, and grabbed my new royal blue pumps, since I made the mistake of wearing nice shoes at work only once. I called and requested a taxi to pick me up in twenty minutes, as I was in no condition to drive and was secretly hoping not to need a car after arriving at my destination. After applying my makeup and singing along to a medley of pop songs on the bedroom clock radio, I covered my weird hair color with a black fedora, slipped into my leather jacket, and shoved keys, lip gloss, ID, and cash into the pockets as I locked my door. I was excited, and it felt good.

The cab dropped me off on Fourth Avenue just short of Broadway, and as I rounded the corner, I saw what used to be the old Merchant's Hotel. It was now a several-story restaurant. Most of the strip was cluttered with souvenir shops and touristy bars with live music and fried pickles. But this place stood out. I had never actually been in there but had always wanted to check it out. I saw Robert immediately. He was smiling at me, the corners of his eyes crinkling and his sexy teeth sparkling. When I reached his side, he kissed my lips lightly, put his hand on my shoulder, and whispered, "You look beautiful."

I felt it, too.

We walked through the front door, past the diners seated by the windows, and straight to a hostess stand in the back.

"Two for upstairs please."

"Yes, Mr. Reid."

Robert's voice sounded like butterscotch, and he smelled amazing, like a warm tropical breeze, which contrasted with the cool winter's night odor de Grant, which I'd sort of gotten used to. And his jeans were just tight enough, and his blue button-down shirt looked fantastic with his eyes. I noticed a Rolex on his left wrist.

We took the elevator to the second floor. The ride was a little awkward since the hostess was riding up with us and making eyes at Robert. He wasn't making them back, but still. Everything felt better when the doors opened and he put his wide hand on the small of my back and led me in front of him. The hostess had to ride down alone. Ha. My knees were so wobbly, I felt like I was going to fall right off of my new heels.

We sat next to the window overlooking Broadway. The only other lighting was small twinkling candles placed around the room and a dim chandelier in the middle of the room. The waitress brought over a silver bucket on a stand with champagne in it and poured us each a glass.

"Fancy," I blurted and quickly regretted it. *Show some friggin' class, girl!*

"I have a weak spot for champagne," Robert said.

"I have a weak spot for mac 'n' cheese gnocchi," I said after the menus were passed out and I had a chance to study one.

"You'll have to let me taste some." He smiled.

My heart sped as I thought of his lips on my fork. I felt warm. I unzipped my jacket and put it on the back of my chair, and I thought I caught Robert sneaking an admiring peek at me.

"I'm surprised you got my e-mail, since it's a weekend and I sent it to your work address," I said.

"BlackBerry," he explained. "I'm always available. Have to be."

We chatted about inconsequential things that suddenly mattered, like where we went to school and what sports he played and what instruments I tried to learn—

badly, to the distress of my otherwise musical family. By the second glass, the bubbly was starting to go to my head, and we began to talk about relationships. Robert had never married, had no kids, and was not seeing anyone special.

"So I take it you are not with that cop anymore," he said.

"Did I tell you about that?" I wondered aloud.

"It was in a news piece we did about L'Affair Hopewell."

"Do you remember every article you read?"

"Pretty much," he said. "Photographic memory. Technically, it's called eidetic memory. I remember most of what I read. I was tested for it in college."

"I'm impressed. I can't remember people's names without a mnemonic trick of some kind."

"So?" he said.

"So?"

"The cop?"

"Oh!" I said. "Oh, no, that's over. I ended it. Well, actually he did. But I wanted to."

I was getting nervous and tongue tied. Thankfully, my gnocchi and Robert's sea bass arrived. Conversation slowed a little while we savored our dishes. Then Robert broke the silence.

"What happened here?" he asked, running his finger diagonally along a scar across the back of my forearm. I figured that telling him about being attacked with a knife by Mollie Baldwin's little girl was not great first date material.

"Oh, nothing," I said. "I was attacked by a poodle."

"Really?"

"Yep."

"Do you like dogs?," he said. "They're very sensitive to how we react to them."

"Uh-huh. I'm just allergic to them. You have any scars?"

"Nothing that impressive. I cut my pinkie once with a jackknife."

He held it out for me to examine. If I hadn't just filled my mouth, I'd've kissed it.

We decided to skip dessert since we were stuffed and fully carbonated. Without waiting for the bill, Robert handed his card directly to the server—who had referred to herself as our waitress—making her angry and delighted at the same time. She returned quickly. Too quickly. The night could be ending.

Robert excused himself to go to the bathroom. While he was gone, I opened the slender black case and noticed he'd left a very generous tip.

Was there *anything* wrong with this guy?

He took a little longer than Grant used to, but I guessed that the amenities here were a little better than in the Kentucky Fried Chicken loo.

We led ourselves to the ground floor, and as Robert opened the door for me, I noticed a framed certificate boasting "Voted Best Fine Dining 2011 by the *Nashville National*." Robert saw me looking at it and gave a sly smile that revealed a sexy dimple, which I'd never noticed.

It was a gorgeous night out. The music poured out onto the street, and there was a slight breeze coming from the nearby Cumberland River.

"What should we do now?" Robert said.

"I may have to walk off that gnocchi."

"Fair enough," he said and grabbed my hand.

Suddenly I was out of my body and looking at us holding hands and strolling down the Nashville streets. I could not wipe the stupid grin off of my face. We came up on the Hermitage Hotel, where a group of people was huddled around, taking pictures and listening to a tour guide tell what sounded like a ghost story.

"Oh, this is great!" Robert said. "Have you ever been on the haunted history tour?"

"No. I just recently heard about it, though."

We tagged along with the group, but by our third stop my feet were killing me. Stupid heels. I explained the situation to my date, who grabbed my hand and led me around the corner to Printer's Alley. Before I knew it, we were in the Bourbon Street Blues and Boogie Bar.

"Wait here," he said, putting me at a table for two and tipping the waiter.

"Robert, wait—"

"Just stay there." He smiled, running out the door.

I looked around the room, avoided making eye contact with the single men   or the married men pretending to be single or not caring, because they were in Nashville for a convention and a good time. I was tipsy, I was tired, I was swooning, and I was surprised when Robert came back holding a white plastic bag.

"Give me your foot," he said as he kneeled down.

I placed my foot on his knee while Robert pulled out a pair of fluffy white spa slippers with HOTEL INDIGO sewn on them. I felt like a fairy-tale princess.

As if reading my mind, Robert looked up at me and said, "A perfect fit, Cinderella."

Chapter 9

The next morning I was a little hungover and a little grumpy.

Robert hadn't asked me to go home with him or driven me back to my charming abode or done anything after whistling for a taxi that someone was just getting out of, putting me in it, and handing the driver a twenty.

I spent the entire ride and part of the rest of the night wondering if I'd done something wrong.

Maybe he's just a gentlemanly Southerner, I told myself. Or maybe he went back to hang with that hostess. Or maybe he had someone waiting for him at the Hotel Indigo. Or maybe he had to go to the office. He had just taken a call on his cell. It could be anything.

None of which, not a stitch of it, is any of your business, I reminded myself. *He took you to a nice dinner. Be grateful.*

For what? my angry girl brain asked. He took pity on a lonely lady and had some time to kill. Obviously, the money meant nothing to him.

It went on and on like that till I fell asleep. The cats woke me up to eat. I fed them carelessly, spilling part of their kibble on the floor. They left it there. They had their standards, and they were probably higher than mine.

You threw yourself at him, I chastised myself as I dressed.

No, you didn't. You initiated the kiss good night. Nothing else.

Right. That obviously didn't have enough pizzazz to get him to go further.

The last thing I needed was to run into a conflict at the deli. So, naturally, that was the first thing that happened. It was Dani again. I fought through a larger than usual crowd waiting to get in and ran right into the needle I had managed to find in the vast haystack of the unemployed.

"Oh, Nash, I want to tell you, but I can't," Dani blurted.

"Okay, fine. Then why are you standing in my way?"

"Because I have to," she said. "I did something."

"What?"

I noticed Thom's hands were washing themselves with imaginary water. That was something she did only when she was really, *really* anxious. This time I stopped to listen.

"What's going on?" I demanded.

"Nothing, really. I'm not sure. Maybe it did, but it stopped. Mostly."

"Dani, start making sense!"

"The newspaper," she said.

"What about the newspaper? Dammit, what did you do?"

"I—I posted something. I took it right down, but I—I—"

"What did you post?"

"A picture," she said.

Oh, shit, I thought. "Of?"

She made a squirmy face and answered sheepishly, "The truck."

"The bread truck," I said. There was disbelief in my voice, my expression, in every part of me.

She nodded once. The rest of the staff was looking on, like the gawkers outside the other day.

"Inside or outside?" I asked.

"Both," she said, then added quickly, "I thought it would drive traffic to the site, and it did! We have over two thousand fans!"

"You took pictures of the truck," I said.

She stood still, like I was Medusa. To tell the truth, I felt like a Gorgon right then.

"You put them on Facebook," I went on.

She still didn't move.

"People saw them and became fans of the sight. And?"

Thom rapped on the counter. She held up the front page of the *Nashville National*. The photos were there, on the front page.

"What time did this happen? The Facebook thing?" I asked Dani.

"About seven o'clock," she said. "They were down by nine. Just a couple of hours."

That happened to fall right in the middle of my dinner. Dani's post was what had ended my evening. Someone had called Robert and told him. They'd copied the photos. He wanted to get there and decide what to do—either to screw me or to screw me.

"I know it was dumb, sort of," she said, "but I did it for the deli. I really did. I didn't think it was a big deal."

"Well, how about if *I* think it's a really big deal?" I yelled. "Get out."

"Huh?"

"Get. Out. You were hired to help me, and all you've done is trip me up!"

"Hey, that's not fair!" Dani protested. "I gave you good ideas!"

"Get out!"

Thom came over. "Nash, she messed up, and she knows it. Let it go. We need her today. We can look at this fresh tomorrow."

I turned. "Thom, the bloody truck is on the bloody front page of the newspaper! Probably on its Web site, too."

"Yup!" Luke said.

Dani shot him an angry look.

"Bad call," Thom said. "We all make 'em sometimes. That's how we learn."

I exhaled loudly. I looked back at my office. "Do what you think is right," I said. "You know where I'll be."

I left and shut the door and sat heavily and cried. I didn't know why or about what, exactly. It was just something I needed to do. When I was finished, I looked up the committee list on my computer, got the number for the *Nashville National,* called, and asked for Robert Reid.

He took my call. I was impressed.

"There's just one thing I want to ask you," I said. "Is that why the night ended so suddenly?"

"Yes," he admitted.

"Well, that's a relief," I told him.

"Gwen, I didn't really have a choice—"

"Give me a big fat break," I said. "You're the publisher."

"Exactly! I'm a member of the fourth estate first and foremost. Always have been. Our Web editor found it. I couldn't kill it. That would have been suppressing news."

"What happened to your mission of projecting a certain family-friendly image for Nashville?"

"Sometimes a story has to take precedent. It's always a tough call."

"Sure. Sales had nothing to do with it."

"Truthfully, they don't. A one-day bump doesn't mean much to our bottom line or to our advertisers," he said. "And that's all we'll get from this. You've got to believe me. It would have been irresponsible not to run something everyone was going to be talking about."

"Responsible yellow journalism," I said. "I like that."

"Call it whatever you want," he replied. "We're just a part of the dissemination process. It will be all over the Web and local TV today."

"Aw, great."

"Thank your page administrator."

"It's not *my* goddamn page!" I snapped. "I didn't authorize it."

"You didn't take it down."

He was right about that. And there I was, just the other day, laughing about how scandal is entertaining in the third person. I suddenly felt like Angelina Jolie, but without the kids, money, or Brad Pitt.

"For the record," Robert went on, "your non-page is doing insanely well."

"Among lurid, perverted thrill seekers," I said.

"Maybe. But even lurid, perverted thrill seekers have to eat. And in this economy, be glad you've got that."

"Thank you, Father Reid, for the beatitude."

"You *should* thank me."

"For what? Are you glad for your bank account in this economy? Does that make all your troubles go away?"

"I'm grateful every day, you bet," he said. "That's why I give so much time to the community. And *obviously,* it doesn't make my troubles go away. I have this one now. I've had it for about fifteen hours. It's like a knife in my chest."

I was silent. He was making sense.

"Gwen, you can stay mad or get madder, but I've

gotta tell you this 'poor me' act is getting tired. You know, I knew your uncle pretty well. Ate there when I'd come home from college. I interviewed him in my cub reporter days. He had some setbacks when he first came down here. A hate incident involving swastikas and paint. Windows broken on the anniversary of Kristallnacht. Thom was mugged for what her attackers called blood money. That was just the first few weeks, before he had any kind of client base, but he toughed it out. He understood that the people who did this were freaks, morons on the fringe of decent human society. He realized that running handed them a victory. My dad reported on those stories, too. Front page. Helped find the three idiots who were responsible and put them away."

"I wasn't comparing you to those kinds of people," I said feebly. I didn't know any of that about Uncle Murray or Thom. I felt small and ashamed.

"I know you weren't. The 'beatitude' is about gratitude for surviving when all around you are hurting, but also about not letting yourself be intimidated. Not by rubberneckers, not by the media, not by the police, not by Brenda Silvio, and not by me."

Ridiculously, stupidly, the crime-solving corner of my brain raised its hand. "You know Brenda?"

"Quite well. McCoy's has been a fixture in this town for a lot of years."

"What kind of person is she?"

"Hard worker, pretty good businesswoman."

"I mean off the clock."

He hesitated. Like someone trying to say something nice about someone who wasn't. "She came to the family business after a failed stab at acting in New York and then Los Angeles. Got the looks for it. Don't know if she had the talent. I saw her in a community theater production of *Sweeney Todd,* as Mrs. Lovett. She wasn't bad. But 'wasn't bad' doesn't cut it in the big leagues."

"Bitter?"

"I wouldn't say that. There's a kind of disappointment around her, I guess you could say."

I wondered if she had a dog. I didn't ask. Robert would know what I was hinting at, and that would rev him up all over again. Besides, he probably wouldn't know if she had one or not. Though I was curious.

"You okay?" he asked after a long silence.

"I don't know," I admitted. "I'm sorry I ragged on you, but this is just one more spotlight I didn't need."

"I hear you. I don't blame you. This is a tough situation and a tough case. Just so you know, our crime reporter has come up with zilch, and he's got sources the police don't have. They've also come up with nada."

Which was probably why Officer McCoy was frustrated and Grant was frustrated, and that was all going to get worse before it got better. Like it or not, this was going to be on a low burn for a while.

I had to think about what Robert had said. I told him I didn't feel like talking any more right now, and he said he understood. We hung up not enemies, though I wasn't happy that I'd had to set a bonfire to the logs that could've been used to build a new relationship. I wasn't looking forward to seeing him later; I knew that.

I rolled my rickety chair to the door, stuck my head out from the office, and called Thomasina in.

"Favor?" I asked.

"Sure."

"Can you do the Reid gig tonight without me?"

"I told you, we can manage."

"Maybe A.J. Two can come in—"

"Already had her on notice, just in case."

"In case what? I flipped out?"

"Or fired someone."

I grinned. "I love you. You know that?"

"You should."

"I do."

"I'm takin' Dani."

"I thought you might."

"You thought right."

"Hey, Thom? You never told me you were mugged in the service of my uncle."

Her good humor seemed to ebb, momentarily leaving her face a silent mask. "I don't like to talk about it."

"Make an exception?"

She shifted her weight, like a boxer dropping his defenses. "I was closing up, and three guys pushed their way in. Called me names, took my purse, and slapped me to the floor. I called the police when they left. Your uncle met me in the hospital. Just a few cuts, nothing serious. The worst of it was while he was trying to comfort me, I was trying to explain to him that this wasn't Nashville. This wasn't even the South. It was just three losers. He understood. Made us strong, together. Nothin' beat us after that. Not slow times, not weeks when neither of us took our wages . . . nothin'."

"Thank you for sharing that," I said. "And for what you did."

She smiled warmly. "What doesn't kill me—"

"Makes me stronger," I said, finishing.

Ironically, it was a saying of Nietzsche, the philosopher beloved by the Nazis. Though I knew it from the Schwarzenegger movie *Conan the Barbarian,* which was a favorite of Phil's. Maybe Robert was right. In the heart of that mess—the divorce, not the movie—I had felt I'd never see daylight. And I did. Not where and how I had expected, but it came. All I had to do was put one foot forward, then the other, then the next. . . .

Thomasina straightened and said she'd take care of the two-hour gig. I felt a little guilty dumping this on the team, but then, they *were* a team, a good one despite the blips that made me crazy, and . . . what the hell. I was the boss. That's what bosses get to do.

I worked in my office through most of the morning service, paying bills and periodically checking in with the staff and grabbing a few Diet Cokes, mostly for the caffeine. I was fighting the urge to eat a fried bologna sandwich, since I'd made a deal with myself that the generous slice of Johnny Cashew pie I was planning on eating would be dinner. Finally giving in to my craving, I went out and prepared to slap two slices of Hebrew National kosher bologna on the grill. As I stood there, I happened to glance out the front door and saw the woman again, the very thin one with the big hat, whom I'd seen out here . . . Christ, I couldn't even remember whether that was yesterday or the day before. Whatever. She wasn't hovering like a banshee across the street now. She was standing right outside my restaurant, like Death not taking a holiday.

I had a feeling she wasn't part of the circus that had been playing since the bread man lefteth. As Thom watched me warily, I opened the door slightly and popped my head out.

"Can I help you?" I asked.

"Gwen? You are Gwen Katz?"

"Yes."

The woman smiled thinly. She looked like she might have been beautiful once. She still might be, if she put a little meat on her frame and did her nails. Her fingertips were rough. She worked with them somehow. My aunt, who worked in the garment district, had slightly dark, rough fingers like that.

"I saw you on the news, and I had to come down and meet you in person," she said with a gentle Southern lilt.

"Sorry. I'm not giving autographs," I told her. I was wrong. Sue me. She *was* part of the circus.

Or so I thought.

"That isn't why I'm here," she said.

And then this woman whom I had never seen or spoken with or heard of said something that caused my sore feet to go numb, all the way up to my hips, and my brain to cloud from my skull to my lower jaw.

"My name is Lydia Knight," she said softly. "I am your late father's mistress."

Chapter 10

All I could do was stare at her, at Lydia, as she sat with obvious familiarity at my desk. She had seen it before, she said, many times. I didn't want to think what else she might have done on it. She smiled with recognition at the photographs. She even knew which part of me—my ears—I got from my father.

She was in my chair, I was standing with my back against the closed door, and I had warned everyone to stay away. I had warned I would be listening for footsteps. If anyone stopped, I swore I would use my letter opener to stab whoever was there.

I was too stunned to react. In fact, I didn't know what I had left to react *with*. I was in emotional dry-heave territory.

Lydia was what they called a handsome woman, with strong cheekbones and white hair pulled tight like that of Peter Parker's aunt May. In fact, that was who she looked like, only more elegant. She was slender, but she didn't seem weak. Her slow, deliberate movements were a matter of genteel Southern breeding, not infirmity.

"When I first met your father, he was slouchin' forward on a bar stool in the Bluebird Cafe, his ice-cold

Schlitz beer in his right hand, and he was just sittin' and starin' at their big ole television set. Well, big in those days. I was there that night to catch Kathy Mattea, before she went gold, and I spotted your father in the back, waitin' for the replay of the Kentucky Derby, the one where Swale ran away with it."

I wanted to tell her to lose the stage setting, but I was too stupefied to talk.

"Your pa just looked so pathetic all alone, completely unaware of the crowd beginning to pour in around him, like he'd been there all day and night, like that statue of the thinkin' man, and no one was gonna move him. And I can still see his adorably ridiculous glasses and side-burns! So I sauntered on up to him and asked, 'Are you from Kentucky, mister, or are you just fond of horses?' He turned. 'Not a big fan of the program tonight,' he said, then smiled. 'Present company excluded.' Well, that got my attention, and we got to chattin' some. I told him that I was originally from West Virginia, right on the border of Kentucky, and that I'd often gone to see the races as a kid before moving here in my teen years.

"I don't suppose he seemed too impressed, although it took a few minutes for him to realize that he'd missed the replay on account of our conversation. But he didn't seem too upset by that, either, so I assumed I was doin' all right by him. Soon Miss Kathy started her set, and we left the café on account of the noise interruptin' our fairly decent discussion. About what I don't recall. But we spent the night walkin' the streets and talkin' about his dreams of doin' somethin' meaningful, somethin' wonderful with his brother, somethin' special. That was over twenty-five years ago." Her gray eyes seemed to stare through the door. "And just look at the deli now."

"It's the eighth wonder of the world," I said.

"Your pap did that, too," she said.

"What?"

"Got sarcastic when someone said somethin' nice about him. Don't ride yourself," Lydia chided.

I almost said, "What? Are you my mother?" but stopped myself. That would have been creepily inappropriate.

I told myself to stay calm, think this through, not react. Because reacting right now would be overreacting, like slapping this bitch into last week. My dad had a right to a private life here. He was separated from my mother, even though they never divorced. But this was still seriously, uncomfortably strange and definitely unwelcome. Oh, and really bad timing.

"I'm sure you have a million questions, my darlin'. I know I do. It's been nearly thirteen years since I lost your father, and he left such a big hole in my heart. And an even bigger one in my life. I've worn black every day since his passin', and since we never got hitched, I've been one step short of strugglin' to stand on my own two feet. He was always quite the provider. Early on we moved in together into a two-story colonial home. He split that halfway up the middle with Murray, your late uncle."

What? I thought. He lived with her in what was now my house?

Something knotted deep down. I had a bad feeling this part of the story was just a preamble. God help her if she made a move to try and kick me out.

"We had such wonderful times there," she went on gaily. "And Murray, God rest his soul, was always drummin' up somethin' new for us to all do together, on the town, at all hours of the night. Your daddy said he hadn't had as much fun since his time in the air force when he was stationed in Germany. I always loved to hear him tell those stories, didn't you?"

No. It was always about him. That was what my mother said.

"You know he had a lady there, too?"

Okay . . . time to shut up, Lady Lydia.

"It was this local girl he'd always sit next to on the bus on his civilian rides into town. He'd always offer her a stick of gum, he said. And she'd always accept. Until one day he didn't have any regular chewin' gum, only that laxative-type gum, but he didn't want to disappoint her, so he offered her that, and she accepted. Well, their many afternoons together ended after that bit of business. Can't blame her, really."

Thank goodness my mother has passed on, because this gal's monologue would've stopped her heart.

"I hope you don't mind that I'm tellin' you all of this. I know it's a lot to take in and I'm blabbin' at the mouth, but I've just been dyin' to get to know you for years, and I wasn't sure until I saw you on the news the other day that it was actually you runnin' this establishment."

She finally stopped talking. So I said, "I'll admit I don't know what to say. It's a little shocking, to say the least."

"A little like finding a live dead body, I'd imagine," she said.

"I guess," I replied. That was almost a Dani-ism. "You know, I didn't know he had a girlfriend. I probably should have guessed."

"Well, it wouldn't be something for a proper lady to think about, would it?"

I didn't bother to explain that that did not apply. At all.

"I know how you must feel. Your father having a secret kinda life and all. But he was dead set on never divorcin' your mother, even though they were never going to live together again. Of course, your daddy was heartbroken when your mother passed in ninety-nine."

Don't mention my mother, you witch. Don't.

"To tell the truth, I imagined that her death had something to do with his own passing later that same year, like they were soul mates separated by a quirk of him not wanting to work for her father."

"It was a little more complicated than that."

"So I've heard. Still, it was all very sad. Very sad indeed. He never really got over it. And I never really got over him."

Okay, no more trips down memory lane, please. It was time for her to go. My dad didn't care enough to introduce us, so why should I waste any more of my time? She'd already unpacked enough skeletons to choke a snake.

"He was a gifted man, though," Lydia said, pressing on, "who, like his idol John Wayne, lived by a code of conduct. Take care of your family, take care of your friends, don't step on too many toes, and do what you can to help the rest of the world. In your father's case, he provided the people of Nashville with many a full belly."

And, I wondered, what did my amazingly wonderful father leave you with? A bellyful of memories and a whole lot of sadness, apparently.

"And as for me," she said, "I may not have gotten a house or the business or even an honorable mention in his will, but at least he gave me Stacie."

Thinking back bitterly to Robert's rottweiler, I said, "Who's that? Your dog?"

"Your sister," she said.

My what? I couldn't say those words or any other words, for that matter. It was as though I'd poured paste down my throat.

"You have a sister, Gwen. Stacie. There! I said it again! Oh, it feels so good to tell you after all these years. Your father and I had a daughter. He named her

Stacie, after your great-grandmother Sonia. She'll be twenty-three this May."

"I have a what?" was all I could say.

"I know it's a lot to take in, but I felt it was time for you to know."

"Why? Because you saw me lying on the street with Candy Sommerton? Was that one of the prophecies that needed to be fulfilled?"

"No, because your father forbade me to tell you! It wasn't up to me. He kept a lot of things private, separate."

"In all the letters he wrote, in the yearly visits I made here, what did he do? Hide you then?"

"I stayed at a motel," Lydia said. "He visited me when he could."

"Oh. That's why I spent so much time flying solo with Uncle Murray. Got it. So in all that time, at his funeral . . . Were you there, too?"

"In the background, where no one could see."

"Right. So with all that history between you . . . Wait. Did his lawyer, Dag Stoltenberg, know?"

Lydia nodded.

"Jesus. So the four of you knew, and three of you survived him, and no one once thought, Hmm, gee, maybe we should tell Gwen she's got a *little sister?*"

There were footsteps outside the door. "Get lost!" I shouted. They scuffled away.

"I wanted to tell you, sweetie, but understand that he was so proud of you, going to college and studyin' things an' all. He didn't want you to feel pressure, like you had to be here instead of there. Like you were missin' out on somethin' or had to take care of me or Stacie. And then, gradually, it just became easier to say nothin' rather than come clean. I figured it was somethin' we'd get to one day."

"Well, lucky me! Today's that day!"

Lydia fussed with her fingers as though she was twisting an imaginary handkerchief. "Maybe he was right. Maybe comin' here was a bad idea. I should go."

"No! *Not* telling me was the bad idea."

"Well, there was another reason, too," Lydia went on. *No,* I thought. *I don't think I want to hear this.*

"While your father was a big part of Stacie's life, I don't think either of us were ready to be responsible for a child. Not on his catch-as-catch-can salary augmented by a deli worker's wages. He was separated, and I was twice divorced, no alimony, and workin' in a shoe store as a clerk."

That explains the fingertips, I thought. *Slipping feet into shoes day after day.*

"As it was, Stacie spent most of her time living at Auntie Thomasina's. I don't know what we would have done without her."

What? That was bombshell number . . . I didn't even know. I'd lost count.

"Thomasina?" I blurted. "Thom, Thomasina?"

"Yes, God bless her."

"She knew?"

"She was our savior."

Well, wrap and bow tie me, as Thom herself was known to say. That would explain why my dear friend had told me she didn't know my dad well. That was a safer play. If she didn't talk about him, she couldn't slip up. That would also explain why Thom had gone out the back door as Lydia had come in the front. Newt was the one who usually took garbage to the Dumpster. Besides, Thom hadn't been carrying anything except herself.

I couldn't believe what I was hearing. Not only did my father have an illegitimate daughter, but my closest friend raised her! And neither told me about it! Better yet, both decided *not* to tell me about it! The ripples of deceit were too great to comprehend at that moment. I just had to keep twisting the napkin in my hands and tumble to the bottom of this chilling, mind-numbing chasm.

"Hey, Lydia . . . a question."

"Of course, darlin'."

"Did you happen to know a man named Joe Silvio?"

"Why, why do you ask?"

"Why-why is because Nashville is apparently like one of those charts on *The L Word* about who slept with who."

"Dear, what *are* you talkin' about?"

"Just . . . humor me. Did you know him?"

Lydia sat a little more upright, as though bracing for a fight. "I did, yes."

"Of course you did."

"A lot of folks down here knew him," she said. "Churchgoin' folks."

Was that a dig at my not being among those? Who cared? This woman's opinion didn't matter.

"Explain," I said.

"He was a highly visible member of the Belmondo Church on Music Square East," she said. "He ran an equipping class."

"A what?"

"A gathering at the church that helps people cope with life using Bible lessons and prayer. I went from time to time as the stress of life wore me to a nub. I saw one of your customers there."

"Who?"

"A woman who was on TV with you," she said. "A plus-size woman with hair not quite the color your own was when I first saw you."

"Big Red?"

"She was with two other women."

"Big Red," I said.

"And that reporter," Lydia went on. "She knew him, too."

"Which one? Candy?"

"That's right. Candy Sommerton," Lydia replied. "She did a report about the group . . . oh, about two weeks ago. I saw that on the television."

I was taking all this in, though I still had the biggest problem wrapping my tired brain around the idea of a house of worship on Music Square East. In New York we had churches on Trinity Place and John Street. Though I guess St. Patrick's on fashionista Fifth Avenue would seem strange to some people. But I digress.

"Getting back to your father . . ."

Must we? I thought.

"I wish things had gone differently," Lydia said. "I sincerely do. But I'm no mother. And your father, God rest his soul, is lucky he got you to turn out so good."

"That was my mother's doing," I said, standing up for someone who had no say in this tawdry matter.

"I'm sure it was partly that," Lydia said.

"No, it was *all* that," I replied. "I loved my dad, but like you say, he was no father. He was pretty MIA for most of my life, and he never once came to see me in college."

"Maybe so, but he was proud of you always," Lydia said.

"That's great to hear," I said. "Just great. Listen, Lydia. I've enjoyed this *so* much, but I really need to get some work done and sort things out in my brain."

"Of course," she said, rising. "I have to get home, too. I'm still at the shoe store, as manager."

"Good for you." It sounded cranky, not complimentary. As intended.

"I have to walk the dog and get to work."

Now my shoulders went up. "You have a dog?"

"A wirehair fox terrier." She smiled. "It's really Stacie's. I keep it for her. Lively thing, even though he's ten. He gives *me* a brisk twice-daily walk."

"How nice for you both."

"It is," she said, missing *that* sarcasm.

"They jump pretty high, don't they?"

"Oh, yes."

I smiled a big fake smile. A lot of people in Nashville had dogs, a lot of people apparently knew Joe, and a whole bunch of folks probably had both of those on their personal résumé. Still, looking at her little white teeth through her little red smile, I *so* wished that this vamp was also a vampire.

She took a pen and a piece of scrap paper from her purse. "My cell phone number," she said, writing it down. "In case you wish to talk."

I didn't thank her. I had no intention of ever using it.

She laid a tender hand on the desk as she stood. Her fingers lingered there a little longer than they should have. I counted to three. And failed to stop myself. I looked sharp little knives into those dull gray eyes.

"Aren't you ashamed by all this?" I demanded.

"Pardon?"

"Isn't there some part of you that regrets all this subterfuge and web spinning and bullshit?"

My words did not draw blood. "Love makes us do the unexpected," she said.

"Like getting pregnant."

"A moment of passion," she replied.

"Oh, please," I moaned. "There was a morning after. Did you not think of the consequences? The responsibility?"

The woman's face grew cloudy. "Do not lecture me, girl."

"My office, my rules," I shot back. I wasn't in the mood for mouth. Not now and certainly not from her.

"*Your* office," she said with the hint of a smirk. She recovered herself, once again becoming the wannabe Southern lady. "My only thought, dear—and perhaps you will experience that one day yourself. . . . I surely hope so—was to retain a piece of your father in case he ever went away. That I have done. Stacie is a living embodiment of us both, something our love created."

"And your lifestyles abandoned," I said.

"We were not perfect, girl."

"Stop calling me that. I'm a woman."

"Then behave like one," she said. "You're acting spoiled, like a child."

Wow. Another lecture from someone else who knew what was best for me. That was okay by me. I was ready for a fight.

"How would you know what a spoiled child is like?" I asked. "Doesn't sound like you spent a lot of time with your daughter."

To paraphrase what Marv Albert used to say while covering the Knicks or the Rangers when Phil had them on, "She shoots. She scores!" All formality bled from the woman. Along with blood. Her face was even paler than before.

"You are correct," she said. "I did not spend as much time with Stacie as I wished to. As perhaps I should have. But we wanted her. We loved her. Adoption? Abortion?" She practically spat the word. "It was never a thought."

"So you're a hero to the pro-lifers," I said, unmoved and relentless. "Good for you. That's something else we don't have in common, though I do have to ask . . . Why tell me all this? Did you think we could all have a great big Thanksgiving dinner or maybe have a big Hanukkah-Christmas celebration, all the Katz spawn under one roof? Jeez, I meant the Katz spawn I know about. Maybe there are more. Maybe I have a black sister or brother, and we can add Kwanzaa to the mix—"

"Gwen, stop. Please."

"Why? That would make news. The seasonal trifecta! We can invite Robert Reid and Candy Sommerton!"

"I said *stop!*" Lydia cried. "For God's sake, enough."

I stopped, but not for her. I did it for me. I was spewing now, like one of those pinwheel fireworks I used to get at Coney Island—which I missed very much just then. I wished I was back home, back in time, just starting out before I married, not making all the mistakes I did, which included Phil and working on Wall Street, but being too afraid to jump into some of the investments I recommended for others, and continued right up to last night, when I thought that Robert Reid was actually interested in me and wasn't just a muckraking piece of journalistic garbage.

"All right, Lydia," I said. "I'll stop." Without taking my eyes from the woman, I reached behind me and turned the doorknob. "But we're done here. For good."

Lydia looked away, then down. "You asked me a question a moment ago."

"Forget it. I don't care to hear the answer."

"You must," she said. Then she looked at me. "I mean, I wish you would."

My upper and lower teeth met in a bite that could have gone through my mother's holiday dishes.

"I came here for one reason," Lydia said. "I came here for Stacie. She desperately needs your help."

Oh, that was rich, I thought. Here I was, ready to crack up, but someone needed my help. Yet I have to admit, the woman's admission did tweak my curiosity.

How totally, utterly, tragically sad *that* gal must be.

Chapter 11

Lydia added her daughter's name and number to the piece of paper, then left. I looked at it, wanting to crumble it and toss it in the trash. I just pushed it aside.

Stacie Leah. I wondered if the girl's mother had given her my father's name. My guess was not. From the sound of things, down here twenty years ago, Katz wouldn't exactly have opened a world of opportunity. Even if folks weren't neo-Nazis or racists, there was no reason to give the few and the twisted a homing beacon.

Lydia was gone, but I stayed where I was. I didn't want to talk to Thom, not then—and apparently, she was just as happy to avoid me. It occurred to me that I'd worked so closely with Thom day after day after day and yet these two big, fat parts of her life with the Katz family had remained hidden. It made me wonder what else I didn't know—not just about her but about everyone. For all I knew, Grant could be a cross-dresser like J. Edgar Hoover. Robert could be gay. Dani could spell *Beethoven*.

I sat and thought. Surprisingly, not about Lydia or Stacie or my father. That whole thing made me sick to my very soul. No, I did what any soul-weary deli owner would do in my place: I Googled Joe Silvio.

A couple of articles later I discovered that this guy was everything Lydia had said and more. She had actually left out the best part, which she probably didn't know and which would have been nice for Grant to share with me: The guy had a police record. Petty larceny. Stole a couple of computers from an overnight delivery service where he was a driver. That was how he met his future wife. Brenda's father hired him on some sort of work-release program. I guess they felt the worst they had to lose was a couple of loaves of bread.

A guy steals one computer because he needs it, I thought. *If he steals a couple, it's in order to fence them.* I wondered if Joe still had some of his old larcenous contacts. Maybe he had robbed places he delivered to or had cased them. Maybe he'd been trying to get out of the business and someone hadn't wanted him to.

Not that I should have been worrying about that, Joe, his death, or anything other than the blessings that were already on my table. After a half hour I turned my attention back to what I really should be dealing with—first and foremost, an employee with whom I clearly needed to spend just a little more face time today.

Déjà vu. Once again I inclined my head into the small hallway leading from the main deli area to my office.

"Hey, Thom?"

"Just a sec." She was just making change for A.J.

"No, now, Thom," I said pleasantly.

"I said—"

"I heard you," I said in a singsong voice. "But I really need to hear about the half sister you never told me I had."

There were gasps. I heard them, like little sobs at a funeral. Thomasina stubbornly finished what she was doing. I could see she was not going to be cowed, unlike A.J. and Dani and Newt, all of whom had obviously just pieced together the scenario and seemed about a head shorter than they were the last time I saw them. Maybe because they were ducking down a little in case I threw something.

Thomasina called Raylene over to work the cash register until she came back. She walked over briskly, looking down, not from fear or embarrassment but more like a bull about to gore a torero.

She came in, and I shut the door behind her. She stood where Lydia had stood, with the same proud defiance.

"So?" I said.

"So," she replied. "We're moving on from hate crimes?"

"Don't mix meat and milk," I said. "You raised my half sister. And never told me."

"Did you want to know?"

"Ef, no."

"Okay. Then we're done here."

"I don't think we are," I said.

"No? What do you want to say?"

"How about, 'You could've told me!'?"

"Why? You're mad at your father. I knew you would be. You feel bad for your mom. I knew you would be that, too. You would've hated your . . . whatever the heck Lydia is. I don't even think there's an official name for that."

"Slut. Whore. Jezebel."

"Well, I figured that out, as well. You wouldn't have liked the girl, your half sister, even if she whizzed gold."

Thom was obviously worked up herself. For her, referring to any lower-body function was the equivalent of using a four-letter word.

"You might have given me the benefit of the doubt," I said.

"Honey, it just wasn't my place."

"Well, the catfight's out of the bag now," I said. "Spill."

Thomasina stood there, defiant.

"What?" I asked.

"You don't talk to me like that," she said. "I don't deserve it."

Until she said that, I hadn't realized how tense my shoulders still were. She was right, though. It was everyone else, not her.

"I'm sorry," I said. "Tell me about it. Please."

Her face softened. "Gwen, what I did I did for your uncle Murray. He was in agony over this. Lydia? She ain't nothin' but a hound dog sniffin' for leftovers. She was always miffed that your daddy wouldn't marry her. I think some of that contributed to her giving Stacie to me. I think she did it to hurt your daddy."

"How did that hurt him?"

"It moved her to his brother's circle. It was kinda like a chess move, I always thought. I move the queen here, and you have to move me to you to get her back."

"But she was living with him, she said."

"Except when you came to visit. Or he just didn't feel like having her around."

"So he didn't love her?"

"Oh, he did in his way. But he loved your mother more, too. And he loved himself more than that. I know that sounds harsh, but he really wanted to be by himself, doing his thing. I once heard him say to Murray, 'I didn't leave a good woman to take a bad one.'"

"Did Lydia have a reputation?"

"She was a bit of a wild mare then, she was. At least, that's what folks who knew her said when they saw her here."

"Lydia made it sound like they were so in love. And they were having fun."

"They were! Too much fun to be bothered with a child, however much Lydia went back and forth on that. Some days she wanted a family. Some days she wanted to party. Your uncle and I—we thought it best to just take care of Stacie ourselves. And your father agreed. He had wanted Lydia to put the baby up for adoption, but she wouldn't hear of it. The girl became a kind of lifeline when your father wasn't available. Partly a little dress-up toy, as if Lydia was five years old, and partly a piece of your dad."

"Sounds like a real healthy setup."

"You understand it perfectly."

No longer angry, I looked at Thomasina for support. As usual. At least that balance had been restored to the universe.

"When was the last time you saw Stacie?" I asked.

"Oh, lawsy . . . When your dad passed, she moved back with her mother, and I only saw her occasionally."

"So you don't know anything about her?"

"A little. Mostly that she did not pick up where her mother left off," Thom said.

"I don't follow."

"I heard she joined one of the Belmondo Church missions in Okinawa, Japan, when she turned eighteen. That was about five years ago. I lost track of her for a while, but now she is back in town."

"That figures."

"What does?"

"Another string from a pushpin to Joe Silvio."

Thom made a confused face. I told her to never mind. I looked past Thom at the number on my desk. It was local.

"Well, Stacie may have traveled the world for Jesus, but now she's back," I said. "The question is, what do I do?"

"What do you want to do?" Thom asked.

"I honestly don't know," I said.

"In your heart."

I was breathing heavily, looking inside, not liking what I was seeing. "I need to think about that," I said.

"That's fair, child. This has been a whole lot of hot soup, and poured with a ladle."

Into a bowl that was already full, I thought. I screamed inside at the thought of seeing a face that looked like a mash up of my father and that awful woman. Awful to me, anyway. And apparently to Thomasina. And maybe, I wondered, to Stacie, as well. Could be we had that much in common.

"I've got to get back to work," Thom said. "We've got the Reid thing tonight, and there's still a crowd of thrill seekers. At least they're ordering."

"Always a silver lining, right?"

"If you look for it."

I smirked. "Where's the good in this mess?" I asked.

"I don't know." She shrugged her big shoulders. "Maybe you'll need to talk to Stacie to find that."

A good woman, and wise. I impulsively threw my arms around her. "Thank you, Thom."

"You're very welcome."

"Oh, and one thing more. It's important."

"Yes, hon?"

I stepped back and asked, "Did you happen to see my cell phone?"

Thom seemed relieved to have to deal with something mundane. She said she did not.

I turned toward the kitchen. "Has *anyone* seen my phone?" I yelled, but I was talked out and my voice carried only as far as the counter. The staff heard, though; so did a customer who worked for a moving company.

"Yeah," he said. "I got it right here in my pants."

"Great!" I shouted. "It's set on vibrate! Enjoy!"

He made a disgusting jerking motion on the stool with his hips. Okay, sometimes Southern neighborliness crossed the line. That's why the term *redneck* was invented.

A.J. walked over. "I ain't seen your phone, but there was that police guy came looking for you while you were in with Thom."

"What police guy?"

"The one Grant told to back off."

I didn't ask how she knew what Grant had said behind my closed office door.

"What did he want?"

"To talk to you."

"Did he leave a message?"

"Nope."

"Fine." I didn't give a crap about Officer McCoy. If he wanted to talk to me, he could get a subpoena.

"But then someone else came in."

"Who?"

"I don't know. Never saw him."

"Name?"

"He didn't give it."

"What did he want?"

"Didn't say." She reached into her apron and pulled out a business-size envelope. "But he left this."

"Where? On a table?"

"No. He handed it to Dani."

"Did he have anything to say to *her?*" I took the envelope, ran my fingers along it. No powder inside. Wasn't trying to anthrax me. It occurred to me that I had double the chances of being killed down here than most people: whoever killed the bread man and whoever liked the bread man and thought *I* killed him.

"I asked her that very question. He said, 'Please give this to Ms. Katz.'"

"So he knew my name."

"Apparently. He used it."

"Did Dani say anything else?"

"She said she had seen him before."

"Where?"

"Here."

"When?" This was getting exhausting. I wished A.J. would just anticipate my questions and answer them all at once.

"She saw him the day the bread guy was killed. And the next day, too."

"Was he one of the onlookers?"

"He didn't seem to be, Dani said. See? I did ask relevant questions."

"I appreciate it."

"But you know how Dani is — not the most observant chick in the henhouse. She said the man came in to eat. She remembered him because she had to show him where the bathroom was."

Squinting with the confusion of trivia overload, I slit the envelope. Didn't get a paper cut, which would have been fitting. There was a scrap of paper inside. It had been torn from a yellow legal pad. There was handwriting. Four words in blocky, childish script. They made me want to throw up.

"What's it say?" A.J. asked as she tried to peer over the angled document.

I folded it lengthwise. "A.J., would you get Dani over here?"

"Sure thing. Why?"

"Just . . . please." I said it quietly because I didn't have the strength to shriek the request an octave above high C.

A.J. caught Dani's eye and motioned her over. She arrived, maneuvering deftly through stuck-out chair backs, holding dirty plates. *Pretty well balanced for a newbie,* I thought again. I was also slightly pleased that the deli boss part of my mind was acting independently of my exhausted, barely functioning regular brain. That meant I could literally lose my marbles and still run this place. That was good to know.

"Dani, the man who gave you this note, where was he when you had to show him where the bathroom is?"

"Back there." She jerked a thumb toward my office.

"Swell," I said.

"Why?"

"Nothing," I told her. "Just curious."

"Oh," A.J. said. "I get it. Your phone."

"My phone," I said under my breath. "What did he look like?"

"Just a guy," Dani said. "Young. Black hair. Cute. A little like that host on Channel Five news."

"Bill Roche?"

"That's him."

"Dani, was it him?"

"No," she said. "I don't think so. He was too short."

I didn't bother explaining that it's tough to tell someone's height when they're sitting behind a desk on TV, but there was no point. I walked back to the office and shut the door quietly, because, again, I didn't have the energy to slam, kick, and punch it. Then I dropped the note on my desk and fell into my chair. It complained creakily.

"Don't talk to me," I told the old piece of furniture. "Especially if my dad and that succubus ever used you."

It squeaked.

My elders back in New York—my mother, my *tantes,* their canasta-playing friends, some of the senior execs at the firm—all of them had told me that there are times in life when you truly feel like you've hit a wall. Not when you're young, when you just feel tired. When you're older and you just run out of gas. Literally. Your face feels numb and you drop where you're standing and you don't move again until, like they did with tired horses in the Wild West—according to that Burt Lancaster movie I saw, anyway—they literally light a fire under your belly to get you back on your feet.

Well, this guy had done that. This man who had obviously cased the place for reasons of his own and had gone into my office, pretending to look for the bathroom. He had just lit a fire under my belly with his hastily scrawled note.

It said:

Call your cell phone.

Chapter 12

There was no procrastination. None needed, none given. I picked up the office phone and called my cell number.

"Hello?" the gruff voice on the other end said.

"Hello," I replied. "This is Gwen Katz. The woman whose cell phone you stole."

"I'm sorry about that," the caller said. "I'm sorry it was necessary."

I didn't detect a Southern accent, but then the voice sounded muffled.

"Are you talking through a handkerchief?" I asked.

"Does that matter?"

"I guess not. Just answer one question. Are you Bill Roche?"

"Who?"

"The Channel Five anchor."

"No," he replied.

"Okay. Then what are you? *Who* are you?"

"I can't tell you that," he said. "That's why I took your phone."

"Oh," I said. "Got it." God bless caller ID. Makes for a lot of needless cloak-and-dagger. "So why *am* I calling? Why was it necessary to take my phone, and—just as important—do you plan to give it back? Oh, and do you have a dog?"

The voice on the other end fell silent for a long moment.

"A dog?"

"Yeah."

"No."

"Good. Sorry. I guess that was a lot to throw at a common thief."

"I'm not that," he protested.

"No? Convince me."

"I'll try to, if you'll let me talk."

That was fair. It occurred to me that this was about more than a guy going into my office and taking my phone, which was pretty wrong. It was also about me being mad at my father and transferring that to this guy. "I'll shut up," I told him.

He took a breath. I could hear it amplified by the handkerchief. "I need your help."

"Why me?"

"Because I followed her to you."

"Who?" Christ, it was another game of Sixty Questions.

"Lydia."

Hell's silver bells. I had known that woman for a half hour, and I was already thoroughly sick of her. "What's she to you?"

"Personally, nothing. But she's Stacie's mother," he said.

Another woman I didn't want to hear about. I was hoping this wasn't another ghost of Papa's past. God, I thought, I was just kidding about Kwanzaa . . . I swear.

"I'm listening," I said. "What about Stacie?"

"She needs help."

"I know. I heard."

"No, no, not the kind Lydia was asking for." His voice sounded a little contemptuous. "You lost me. Lydia didn't ask for anything specific."

"Oh."

"What did you think she was going to ask for?"

"Money," the man with my phone said.

"I figured that. Why?"

"Not to help her out, I'll tell you that. Not for bills or debts or anything she could really use."

"Has she got a lot of those?"

"Plenty," the man said. "Her kind of work doesn't really pay."

"I wouldn't know," I replied.

"Lydia wants the money to get Stacie out of town."

My sixth sense was tingling, only I got the feeling I was seeing dead people before they were dead. This time it was my father's other daughter. "Why? Did Stacie do something wrong?"

"I can't say," the man told me.

"Can't? Won't? Clarify."

"Both," he said.

"Does this have anything to do with the dead bread man?"

"Listen, I'm just trying to get you to help someone who was important to your father. And not with money, but with support. She needs that now desperately. She needs a friend."

"We all do. Why should I care? Just because my father had a hand—or whatever—in her manufacture?"

The man was silent for a second. "That's a little cold. You don't even know her."

"And I don't want to," I replied. "Nor have you and your light fingers given me a reason to want to."

"Let's just say there's more to this than just Stacie being caught between a rock and her mother."

"What's the rock?"

"Not what," the man said. "Who."

"Are you the who?"

"I've told you enough," he said. "I'll make sure you get your phone back."

"Thanks, but you haven't told me anything," I pointed out. "You want me to help a woman who means nothing to me and whom I don't want to meet. That's not good enough."

The man was silent again, this time for longer than before. I gave him the time to think. He obviously needed it.

"I'll be over later to explain," he said.

"Why the change of heart? You didn't want to tell me your name a minute ago."

"Scott Ferguson," he said.

"Thanks. What about the 'change of heart' part, Scott?"

"I'll tell you when I see you."

"What time? I may have something important I have to do."

"When do you close today?"

"Six tonight, but I wasn't planning to be here."

"Can you make an exception?" he asked.

His voice was imploring. Also higher, gentler, and more Southern. He'd obviously given up on the bad voice disguise.

"I'll tell you what," I said. "There's something I have to do after the important thing I have to do. I'll see you here at eight. That work for you?"

"It does. Thank you," he said.

"Sure. And don't forget my phone."

"I won't," he promised and hung up.

If I'd succeeded in dying my hair blond, I'd think I was having Alice in Wonderland delusions. Things just kept getting curiouser and curiouser.

I hung up the receiver and stared at my fingers spread out on my giant desk calendar. I experienced an uncharacteristic rush of calm as I inspected my tattered nails. All the oils and sauces from slicing the meats and cheeses, from the salads and side dishes, had left my poor fingers looking like freshly dipped taper candles.

I was relieved that my cell phone wasn't actually missing, and right now even a small victory like that seemed huge. I felt like celebrating and decided that my little candlestick fingers could do with a little nail indulgence at Nail Indulgence on Sixth. I hit speed dial nine. Mei answered the phone.

"Hello, Nail Indulgence," said the treble-pitched, middle-aged woman on the other end of the line. "This is Mei. How may I help you today?"

"Hi, Mei. This is Gwen from Murray's."

"Hello, Miss Gwen. Boy, you been busy!"

"You saw the news?"

"Saw, read, heard, listened to everyone in my shop talking about it. You a celebrity!"

"Lucky me."

"I would like to be famous. Good for business."

"Hey, it's simple. Just find a dead body in your shop."

"I did once. It was a skeleton. It was in a closet, behind a wall."

"Really?"

"Oh, yes. About forty years old. It was a workman who fell from the floor above. No one ever thought to look for him below."

"Wow. I wonder if Grant was on that one."

"Pardon?"

"Nothing," I said.

"What can I do for you today?"

"I was just hoping you had an opening for this afternoon. I just need a basic mani-pedi."

"How is four forty-five?"

I looked at my watch. If I had guessed, I would have said it was already way past that. It was 2:20. "That's good," I told her. "See you then."

"Okay. Thank you. Bye."

I hung up. I put my hair back in a ponytail and tied my scarf back into position and decided I was officially done with phone calls for the day. Done with working for the day. Done with life for the day, at least that part over which I had any control.

With renewed vigor and a sense that maybe things were on the upswing, I stood and went back into the deli. I relieved Thom at the cash register, ignored the stares of sensation seekers, and was so pleasant, the staff obviously thought I'd galloped off the ranch.

No. I had solved the phone mystery, and I'd broken the caller. I had established that I didn't give a spit about Lydia, and that "Queen Solomon" was reserving judgment on Stacie. It had been a good uptick. I was determined to stretch it to an hour of goodness.

I watched as dishes were filled and emptied, customers stood and sat, came and went, chewed and swallowed. Thom was wiping off the menus with antibacterial solution. And a full five minutes went by before my absentminded serenity was interrupted by a courteous-faced Luke.

"Hey, Nash?"

"Hey, Luke. Guess what?"

"What?"

"You can have your open mic night. How's Monday sound?"

"I can't."

That soured my mood a little. I'd just given the kid what he wanted. "Why can't you?" I asked.

"I, uh . . . I have a date. That's what I wanted to talk to you about."

"Your dating life? I thought you had your groupies under control." That amounted to two gals, who I suspected were underage and just hung around for the free beer.

"Yeah, well . . . see, I've kind of been seeing Dani."

"Our Dani?"

"Who else's?"

"Right. But she's only been here for . . ." And then it hit me. "You told her to come here. In fact, you encouraged me to hire her."

"We wanted to be close and sync up our scheds."

"That's how she knew my nickname was Nashville Katz."

He looked way guilty.

I wasn't annoyed. In fact, the two of them had more smarts than I'd given them credit for. "Nicely done. I'd never have guessed."

"No one did. Not even Thom." He grinned. "We put one over big-time, huh?"

"Yeah."

"The thing is, she's upset now."

"Why?"

"She thinks you hate her because she keeps messing up."

"I don't hate her for that," I said.

"You wanted to fire her."

"Yes. Because, like you say, she keeps messing up. But she's got another chance now, right?"

"She does. I just . . . Would you tell her it's okay?"

"What is?"

"Her and you. Your relationship."

"Luke, we don't have a relationship. I'm her boss."

"Yeah, but *we* have a relationship, you and me. We're friends, right?"

There was a certain skewed logic to that. "Sure. Right."

"So can you try and be friends with her?"

"Fine. I'll try."

"Like, now?"

"This second?"

"She's afraid and worried and scared."

"Those are all kind of the same thing."

"I think you should smoke a peace pipe. Please. For me."

My perfect hour was doomed not to reach maturity. "For you, Luke. Send her over."

He practically leaped back to the kitchen, where Dani had been hiding on her break. She came out like Chris Evert when she lost that big one to Billie Jean King in 1971, the match that broke her forty-six-game winning streak. I wasn't alive then, but I had watched it on VHS when I was a kid. That was during the five minutes I thought of becoming a professional tennis player, except that I had no backhand, forehand, or serve.

Long way of saying I knew "beaten" when I saw it.

"Hi," I said when she had managed to schlep over.

"Hi."

"Straighten up," I said, sounding like my mother. I added, as she never would have, "You're not letting anyone see your pretty eyes."

That perked her up a little. She wriggled her shoulders back, like a belly dancer with clothes on.

"Much better. So. I hear you've been dating Luke."

"I love him."

I let that pass. I was in the minority today when it came to women loving men at first sight. I couldn't even get one of them to take me home for a recreational hoedown.

"Well," I went on, "Luke's a little worried that our tiny dustups are going to impact your relationship."

"He's so sweet!"

"Yeah, he is. And I want you to know that that's not the case. He also tells me he's worried that you're worried that I'm going to fire you. I want to assure you that that's also not the case."

"I'm so glad to hear that!" she said. "You were pretty upset before."

"I've been pretty upset since I stepped in that pool of human blood. I think you can understand that."

"I've never done that myself."

"And I hope you never have to. You've been doing a good job here. I watched you bus before. You've got natural talent."

"Really?"

"Really. And no one's complained, at least not that I've heard."

"No one has," she said eagerly. "Except those three ladies that first day."

"That doesn't count. They're pills. We don't care what they say."

"I know, right?"

"Right. I'll tell you what. Why don't we start fresh? I'll try harder, you try harder, and we won't have to yell or be hurt or threaten anymore. Deal?" I offered a big smile across the countertop, then turned to process a credit card A.J. had brought over. A.J. was looking a little sour. Tragically, my new détente wasn't going to spread throughout the civilized world. I wasn't gonna teach the world to sing in perfect harmony.

"It's a deal," Dani said, happier than I could remember ever having seen a young woman. I felt like the Pope blessing an acolyte. It felt good. Maybe the full-hour uptick was still achievable.

Customers came and went, more than usual for a late weekend afternoon. Unfamiliar faces. Looking at me, looking at the kitchen, pointing. Asking if they could go to the back, being told there was no access except through the store or a narrow alley with a gate that they wouldn't be able to open, because I'd put a cinder block behind it and it was going to stay there except for garbage pickup and deliveries.

People got the message. They weren't going back there to look at the murder site. Not even for the twenty that one guy tried to slip me to impress his date.

I noted the hour mark with a private spin of a mental Purim *grogger* and told everyone I'd be back at about half past five. I was sure they were beginning to wonder if I'd ever work a full day again.

At 4:45 I was sitting comfortably in the soft white pedicure chair, thumbing through the latest celebrity gossip magazine. I was daydreaming about who would play me in a movie—I settled on Natalie Portman, even though she was hit and miss and made her best movie, *The Professional,* when she was about thirteen—when someone passed by the shop window, stopped, and stared.

"You know lady?" Mei asked.

"What lady?"

"One outside." Mei pointed with an emery board.

I caught only a glimpse of her as she quickly turned and hurried out of view. She was dressed in well-worn jeans and a button-down blue shirt. She had long brown hair, stood about five-seven—a little taller than me—and was skinnier than anyone who had ever ordered a pastrami sandwich.

But the thing that really grabbed me was her expression. Not her face so much, which didn't shine with anything familiar, but the hungry, restless look of a woman who was searching for something.

I did not get up. I did not intend to give chase. I didn't know *what* I intended to do or what I felt or thought, other than to finish my session here.

Though it was with a combination of rage and curiosity that I said to myself before burying myself back in the *National Enquirer*:

"So that was Stacie."

Chapter 13

What I had to do after I left the nail salon was drive over to Robert Reid's house.

Cars were beginning to fill the sweeping driveway, and I followed the trail of Murray's employees to the back door.

I found Thomasina running the operation like George S. Patton.

"How's it going?" I asked.

"I thought you weren't coming," she said.

I shrugged.

"The working of your mind baffles me," she said.

"I baffle myself," I answered.

I wandered in, pretending to have something to do, checking plates that didn't need checking. I made my way into the kitchen, where I had a good memory to relive. I relived it. I heard Robert's voice coming from the dining room.

"As I helped the governor up, I said, 'Sir, you were supposed to take a stand, not the entire podium!'"

A small group of people laughed. Maybe a little more forcefully than the joke deserved. I couldn't tell; the punch line was amusing enough. I didn't laugh. My face was locked in place. I felt isolated, not just from him but from a world that included governors and people who laughed at jokes. I wanted to show myself in the adjoining doorway, just back against the swinging door and pretend to be doing something else. Let him see me to see how he would react.

I decided against it. What would he do? Either say a platonic hi or ignore me, because he was in social anchor mode. I didn't want either of those. I didn't know what I wanted. I found myself missing Grant just then, which not only wasn't fair to him but also made no sense. I didn't want to be with Grant.

I don't know what I want, except that I just don't want to be so damn alone.

I didn't even feel like I had the memory of my father anymore, sketchy as that relationship was. Whatever I thought we had down here, he'd been holding himself back for another woman.

"Didn't Reagan say something about a podium?" some woman asked.

"That was the nineteen eighty New Hampshire primary," Robert said. "And it was a microphone. The candidate was trying to explain something when the editor of the *Nashua Telegraph* told the soundman to turn off Reagan's microphone. Reagan was angry and said, 'I am paying for this microphone!'"

"Yes, that was it," the woman said.

"But how do you remember that?" someone else said. "You were only what? Three?"

"It's called an education," Robert quipped.

There was more laughter. I wondered if the speaker even realized he'd been insulted.

Talking about politicians sounds interesting, though, I thought. *For that matter, talking about anything but the deli and inventory and employees and dead bodies would be fun.*

In the non sequitur that was driving my train of thought, thinking about bread man Joe made me needle-drop on Brenda Silvio, alone and about as lost as a human being could be. Even my mother, when my father left, pulled up her socks and refused to be depressed—at least on the outside. I wondered what, if anything, was going through this woman's brain. I wondered if I'd judged her too harshly. And, curiously, I wondered the same thing about Lydia. I mean, did it make any sense that I was ready to feel bad for a woman whose husband was murdered but not for a woman who had the misfortune to fall in love with a charming, intelligent, good-looking man who was nonetheless halfway to deadbeat—my dad?

Why does everything have to be so complicated?

Why did my brain have to be so baffling? Was it every woman's brain? *No, Thom is stable. She has her church, she has a stable home life, and she was still able to raise a kid that wasn't even her own!*

Was I more like Dani than I wanted to acknowledge? Is that why I beat up on her? I don't mean the naive, sheltered airhead part, but the lonely girl who wanted a man at the center of her life, even if the fit was obviously flawed and probably wrong. I didn't know much about her, but I knew that her parents were divorced. I'd overheard Luke mention that.

I wasn't going to answer that now. But A.J. Two had been right about one thing. I needed to take a harder look at the things that were troubling me.

I decided to leave before Robert or anyone else saw me. I reminded myself about the reason for the committee meeting. I was thinking clearly enough to know that being here would be perceived as trying to curry favor instead of curry sauce. I had planned on staying in my office when the luncheon was going to be held at the deli.

I thanked Thom and Dani and Luke and A.J.s One and Two for doing a good job and took off. When I thanked Luke, I noticed him wink back at Dani.

Good for them, I thought. Whether it lasted a week or a month or a lifetime, what they had at this moment was working. It was special. It was theirs.

I got back to the deli at 7:30. I microwaved a potato knish, homemade, using my uncle's personal recipe. They were one of the few menu items I made myself. It hit the spot, not just hunger-wise but comfort-wise. I felt like a kid again, at that Coney Island I was missing. I washed it down with burnt, reheated coffee—another taste of New York—just in time for the arrival of Scott Ferguson.

Dani was right: even under the shadowy light of a streetlamp, he *did* look like Bill Roche. Enough to be his brother. I made him out to be early to midtwenties. He was a little over six feet, big shoulders, slightly bowed legs.

I snatched my keys from where I'd plunked them beside the cash register, unlocked the door, and held out my hand.

He went to shake it.

"Uh-uh," I said. I held it out more insistently.

He seemed puzzled. Then he remembered. He reached into what I now saw was a Nashville High football jacket and retrieved my phone. It was dead.

"What would you have done if it hadn't been fully charged?" I asked him.

He reached into his other pocket and gave me the charger. The kid was thorough.

"Come in," I said.

"Thanks."

We didn't introduce ourselves. We knew who we were, and I didn't feel like it.

I put the keys and cell phone by the cash register. I didn't lock the door, in case the kid was crazy or a killer. Given the way things had been going, I wasn't willing to rule anything out. *Were those traces of dog hair on his jacket?*

Now that I had a better look at him, he seemed less photogenic than Bill Roche. He had a two-day growth of stubble, there were charcoal-colored patches under his eyes, and his longish hair looked a little greasy. He also smelled of seasoning.

"Which of my competitors do you work for?" I asked as I motioned to a table. "The Blue Elephant?"

His dull eyes showed signs of life. "How do you know that? Did you go to my Facebook page?"

Lord, what is it with kids and social networking? "No. I've got a good nose. Your boss, Singh, is up for the same Best Mid-Range Restaurant in Nashville Award."

"Oh, yes," the kid said as he sat heavily, gracelessly, like he was in his own kitchen. "He said something about that."

"Really? How bad does he want to win it?"

"What?"

Bad enough to try and pin a murder on me? Does he have a dog?

I was confusing the young man, who already looked a little out of it, so I didn't ask those questions but got back on topic. "Tell me something. Does Stacie know about me?"

"She does."

"Would she be stalking me?"

He seemed surprised. "She's not like that."

"Then why did I see her—at least, I'm pretty sure it was her—outside the nail salon before?"

"Stacie?"

I described her.

He nodded. "That sounds like her."

"So I repeat. Would she have been stalking me?"

"I might have mentioned you were going out. I guess she was curious. Was it about four?"

"Yeah."

"That's when she gets off work. She works at a day-care center, watching kids. Her shift's from seven a.m. to four."

The irony of that was rich and sad.

"So she got off work and stood somewhere outside and watched for me to go. And followed me. That's what stalking is."

"That may be, but I'm not sure she was dead set on meeting you, and I'm also saying that's not who she is. She's not crazy."

"Scott, everyone's crazy. It's just that what brings it out is different for everyone. Like you, for instance."

He looked at me, hurt and puzzled.

"Why the secrecy about your name, about this whole process? Stealing my phone when you could've just asked to talk to me. Wasn't that a little crazy?"

"No. I thought about that. I was concerned because I knew what Lydia was planning on doing, and I wasn't sure how to handle it. I wasn't sure how you'd react. I thought if I had some control over the situation—"

"All right. Never mind," I said. I didn't have time for mea culpas. "Let's agree that she was curious. What's so important? Why does Stacie need two kinds of help?"

"Lydia wants to get her away from here, and I want to help her to stay."

"Because . . . ?"

The kid didn't look like my father. My guess was he was her half brother by some other guy or he was in love with her. I was leaning toward the latter. Lydia would have had to be pretty busy to birth two kids the same age by different men.

"She's my fiancée," he said.

Ah, another burst of love in bloom. God save me from my own cynicism.

"Go on," I said. "Can I get you warmed-over coffee? I'm going to get a refill."

"No, I'm good," he said. He folded his hands in front of him, seemed to be praying as I poured more black coffee in my I'M THE BOSS mug.

"You were saying?" I stated, pressing.

He sighed. "She and I have been together for two years now. I proposed to her six months ago outside the Life and Casualty Tower on Church Street."

"Congratulations." I think I meant it.

"Thanks."

"Does Lydia approve?"

He nodded. I wasn't expecting that. I sat across from him. "Okay, back up the truck. I thought you and Lydia were at odds."

"We are," he said. "About what to do about it."

"About what to do about what *it?*"

He took a long, tremulous breath. He was slumping forward now, actually leaning on his elbows. "Say, you have anything to drink?"

"I'm guessing you don't mean ice water."

"A beer?"

"Yeah. Sure."

I went behind the counter to the fridge. We didn't have a liquor license, but it was after hours and he wasn't a paying customer. I twisted the cap off an Amstel Light and set it in front of him. He put his hand around it, held it for a second, then took a swallow. He aahed and set it back down.

"You were saying?"

He didn't look at me as he said, "I believe Stacie's having an affair."

I stared at his forehead, trying to pull his eyes to mine. He couldn't look at me, couldn't look up, couldn't do anything but take another swig of beer and then go back to his walking dead state.

"What makes you think that?" I asked.

"We live together in a one-bedroom apartment in Antioch," he said. "Starting a couple months back, she disappears for hours at a time. Says she's got babysitting gigs and comes back smelling like cologne."

"Yeah. Not a lot of babies use the stuff."

"I know."

Note to self: no sense of humor. Either that, or the kid was really, really morose.

"After about four months of this I followed her to a house," he said. "A real good house in Hendersonville. You know the area?"

"I know it." *Please don't say what I don't want to hear,* I thought.

"Nice, right?"

"Very. And?" *More teeth pulling. Is everyone in my life suddenly becoming incapable of speaking in complete, informative sentences?*

"I checked the mail in the mailbox. A single dude owns it."

"His name?" My stomach was twisting.

"Stephen R. Hatfield."

Relief. "You're sure he doesn't have family living with him? Or visiting?"

"I followed her the next two times she went. There wasn't no car pulling out, nobody going out for a night on the town. The owner stayed in, and she stayed in."

"Okay, fine."

"No, it isn't," he said.

"Right. I agree. What do you know about him?"

"He owns the building, the whole strip of buildings, where Stacie works. That's probably how they met."

"Okay." I was going to have to coax him along. This was clearly a topic he had no interest visiting. But I had a soft spot for jealousy today, since I was feeling it about my dad's time with Lydia. I decided to be patient. "What else do you know about this guy?"

"He's a powerful man from a wealthy family."

"Powerful how?"

"Doesn't the name mean anything to you?"

"Not off the top."

"You're not from around here."

"No. I'm from New York City."

He lit up a little. "Really?"

"Really."

"I've always wanted to go there, ever since I saw all the news coverage from the World Trade Center. I was a kid, but I remember all those people serving food to the firefighters and first responders. I wished I was up there helping."

I sipped coffee and sat back. Just shows, again, how you can misjudge someone.

"Is that what got you into the food business?" I asked.

He shook his head. "My mom's datin' Mr. Singh."

"Ah. Well, then, back to Hatfield—" I came to a hard stop on the *d*. "Hold on. *Hatfield?* As in the Hatfields and the McCoys?"

"Yeah. See? I figured you heard of 'em."

The whole world and all those *L Word* connections seemed to just get infinitely more complicated. "Everybody's heard of them. You're saying that these Hatfields and the dead man's bakery are *the* feuding families?"

"They are. I did a book report about them senior year, so's I know a lot about them. I have a pretty good memory."

"Me too. I remember all the crap I shouldn't."

He looked at me quizzically. I indicated for him to continue.

"The whole thing started in the seventeen hundreds," he said. "There were the Hatfields of West Virginia and the McCoys of Kentucky. Over the years the Hatfields did better than the McCoys financially. Devil Anse Hatfield's lumber operation was a big hit. Some McCoys worked for him. Anyway, come the Civil War, an uncle of Devil got mad at a McCoy because he joined up with the Yanks. He got a busted leg and was sent home and got himself shot by a Hatfield. It never got proved, though. Things got worse a couple years later, when the families got into a fight over a pig."

How many men would still be alive if they'd kept kosher? I couldn't help but wonder.

"That got another Hatfield shot," he went on. "The hate kept rolling into the eighteen eighties with more killings and came to a head in the eighteen eighty-eight New Year's Night Massacre, when armed Hatfields surrounded a McCoy house and blew it all to hell. Eventually, one guy was hanged, and the whole thing sorta petered out at the turn of the century."

"Do you think it's still going?"

"I don't rightly know," he admitted. "What I do know is that Lydia is afraid of Stephen and wants to get Stacie out of Nashville. I want to get her to stay and stop seeing this guy."

I drank more coffee, thought about what he'd told me.

"What if she did?" I asked. "Would you still want to marry her?"

"With all my heart," he said. "Do you believe in love at first sight?"

"I'd like to," I admitted.

"We met when she was a high school cheerleader and I was a center," he said with his first real smile, "and I've loved her ever since. Because of the way she grew up, with two parents who couldn't seem to hold on to a dime between them, she's always wanted financial security. You can understand that."

"Certainly."

"I understand that and I forgive her, however much what she's doing is like hooking," he said. "In fact, that makes it easier. Knowing she's seeing this guy because he can provide for her, not because she loves him."

An enlightened cuckold. I was even more impressed. "I'm glad to hear that, Scott. We all make mistakes, and maybe this is her big one."

"It really heartens me for you to say that. Because you know what? I want her for my wife, and now I want you for my sister-in-law."

That thought was so unexpected, so oddly chilling, I didn't even react. I was frozen.

"I guess the question is, Scott, what can I do? Didn't you just say she may not be so eager to meet me?"

"Yeah, but that's . . . I dunno. Pride, I guess. You own a place, and she works for an hourly wage watching kids. You've been to college and had a white-collar job, and she was all about ten-person formations and barely made it outta high school. You had an official last name, and she didn't."

"How do you know about my education and job?"

"SearchBug," he said. "You know. People finder."

I didn't know. *Goddamn Internet.*

"Well, it sounds to me like we've got a recipe for disaster," I said. "Because I can't apologize for who I am and what I've done."

"I'm not saying you have to. I *wouldn't* say that. And

I'm not saying you should feel sorry for her, either. She don't."

"Then I repeat, what can I do?"

"Talk to her, woman to woman. Sister to sister."

I wished he would stop that. I wished both of them would. "What am I supposed to do, Scott? Say, 'Hi. I'm your half sister. Nice to meet you. Stop seeing that rich guy'?"

"No, that wouldn't do it," Scott said. "But if you talk to her like you just talked to me, making me feel at ease and all, she'd respond. I know it. She wants someone she can talk to. I think that's half the reason she goes to see Hatfield. She thinks he listens to her."

"You don't?"

He looked at me with the glummest expression I'd seen since intermission at *Starlight Express* on Broadway. "He's forty-three. Newspaper archive says he's been married twice. What's a poor kid gonna say that he hasn't heard before or could give a spit about?"

"Even if that's true, what makes you think she'd listen to a stranger just because she's got some common ancestry?"

"Because she's never had a woman in her life she really respects, other than the one who works for you."

Perfect! I thought. "Get Thomasina to talk to her."

"That wouldn't help. Your lady would lecture her, like she did when she was a girl. Stacie wouldn't take to that." He drained half the bottle of beer. "She needs someone she can respect, who maybe has had some experiences she can relate to."

"Scott, I've never had a relationship with a guy just because he's rich." *In fact, I seem to have a particular problem landing one who is.* "I've never even known a man as long as you two have known each other. And I don't like her mother."

"Neither does she," Scott said. "As mean as it sounds, I was hoping you'd say that. It's something else you would have in common."

I considered that. "Is there some reason, other than your basic abandonment and born-out-of-wedlock issues, that Stacie doesn't get along with Lydia?"

"Yeah," he said. "Not too many months back, she had the misfortune to find out that after she was born, her mom tried to sell her for thirty grand through an adoption agency."

Chapter 14

Well, bombshell number whatever was not the biggest of them all, but it was sure the stiletto-in-the-heart knifiest of them. What was worse was that Scott's little confessional had given me a very, very bad thought—one I did not want to entertain but couldn't get out of my head.

I rinsed my mug, put the beer bottle in the recycling bin, and closed the deli. My head felt like a balloon full of wet sand, something I'd once achieved on the Coney Island beach, thinking it would make a great flotation device. It might have, too, if I hadn't accidentally put a piece of shell in there, which popped it when I went in the water. To this day, really, wet beach sand makes me sad.

I had turned off the dining room lights but had left the kitchen area lights on, as was customary—police bulletin, to help them watch for intruders. Then I put on my tan retro Members Only jacket and went out the front door. There were no gawkers, but I felt that I was another day older and deeper in dreck.

I began my block-and-a-half walk to the parking garage. I was soothed by the sound of my cowboy boots hitting the sidewalk. That was one experience I never would have had in New York, even if I'd worn cowboy boots then. The tall lip of the starchy boot hitting me mid-shin reminded me of the few youthful times I'd gone skiing in Connecticut. Ski boots weren't the easiest way to travel unless they were tucked in skis. The serious heel-toe action and the very little ankle movement in the boots were awkward, but the extra effort was worth it. Worth it knowing no one else could fill these boots quite like me. There was a worthwhile metaphor in that. I was bearing up under a lot. Good for me. And I found myself walking with that same distinctiveness that cowboys were known for, almost like I was leading with my knees and kicking with my hips. If only Mother could've seen me. She'd have rolled her eyes.

I entered the garage and said good night to Randy. The pleasant *clap-clap-clap* of my boots was amplified in the concrete garage. I reached the second floor by the stairs and walked briskly to my car on the far end of the enclosure. I pressed the unlock button on my remote, and it was only then that I heard the clacking of heels from somewhere behind me. I slowed without turning to get a better grasp on the clearly approaching sound.

High heels. I'd heard them before. Walking into my deli. I stopped and turned around.

"Hello, Lydia."

The taut face was tauter still, with anger.

"What did he say to you?" she demanded. She didn't even ask how I knew it was her.

"About what?" I asked. "Your daughter or the fact that you lied to me?"

"Lied?"

"About not considering adoption, about your heart being, oh, so full of love."

The woman stopped about a yard from me. She was

neither repentant nor cowed. "Yes, I considered it. I wanted a good life for my baby, one I could not provide."

"The thirty grand had nothing to do with it?"

"I didn't take it, did I?"

"Why?" I asked. "Love?"

"Yes, love. Think whatever you want of me, but don't ever doubt that I love my little girl!"

I believed her. It wasn't just her passion—which she obviously had an abundance of when properly motivated by a man or child—but I reminded myself that when we spoke, she didn't ask for anything for herself.

"Let's table that for now," I said. "I have a question for you."

"You haven't answered mine."

"He told me about their engagement and their love for one another. Is that true?"

"Yes," she barked.

"He told me he thinks she's having an affair. Is *that* true?"

"We think she is, yes," the woman said. She wasn't quite so huffy about that. It obviously hurt.

"The guy you think she's seeing is named Stephen Hatfield. Also true?"

She nodded.

"That's pretty much all he told me, so here's my question for you. Did you come to the deli to see me?"

"Of course—"

"I mean the first time," I said.

"Why else?"

I moved a little closer. The fluorescent lights weren't the brightest, and I wanted to see her eyes. "Is there any part of your brain that is the tiniest bit worried that her lover put her up to murdering Joe Silvio, wife of Brenda Silvio, née McCoy?"

Her knees swayed like she was doing the Charleston.

I stepped forward and steadied her as a noodly arm went out to the side. She shut her eyes. With an arm around her waist, I opened the back door of my car and helped her sit. I stepped back, looking down at her.

"There's a water in the well between the two front seats," I said.

She leaned on the back of the driver's seat to retrieve it. She popped the cap and took a long drink.

"Let me ask that question another way," I said. "Do you have reason to believe that Stacie did do it?"

She shook her head, still drinking from the plastic bottle. I waited for her to finish.

"There is bad blood between these Hatfields and McCoys," Lydia said. "It has nothing to do with the old disagreements."

"I should hope not, after more than a century."

Lydia looked surprised. "It's been more than a century and a half since the start of the War Between the States. Folks down here are still sore about that."

Score one for the lady in black. "So what is this bad blood about?"

"There have been articles in the newspaper about Hatfield trying to buy the lot that McCoy's Bakery is on. It's the only spot on that street he doesn't own."

"And Brenda didn't want to sell."

"Worse than that," she said. "I was doing a little online research. There is a Web site, Justia, that lets you look up legal documents. McCoy's had just filed a lawsuit accusing him of trying to monopolize the bread business. Seems there are two other bakeries among his holdings, one in Brentwood and another in Mt. Juliet."

That would be Sam's and Alexander's Ragtime Bread. "So we've got what? Antitrust and unfair business practices?"

"Were you an attorney up north?"

That made me mad. I was already studying account-
ing when my dad died. He obviously hadn't felt that was
worth mentioning to his hump puppet. Or maybe he
himself forgot. All of those possibilities stank.

"No, an accountant," I said as calmly as I could.
"Working on Wall Street, those are just terms you get
familiar with." I ticked through the beat points of this
thing. "So you wanted money to get Stacie out of town
in case she's involved somehow."

"Yes. Oh God, she's been a sad girl but never a vi-
olent one. I don't think she's a killer, Gwen."

I still hated hearing my name come from her mouth.

"But you're afraid someone around Hatfield is a
bad guy and she may get dragged in or endangered in
some way."

"Yes."

"Dumb question, Lydia. Why haven't you had this
talk with Stacie?"

The woman looked down at her feet. "She found out
about the adoption."

"How?"

"There was a letter," she said. "It was stuck in a
family Bible, of all things. I left it there, I suppose, when
I was praying for guidance about the baby. Stacie took it
from the top shelf after Scott proposed. She was thinking that it would be fun to have the preacher use a family
heirloom."

"Do you think seeing Hatfield came as a result of
that?"

"I wondered about that," she said. "I cannot dismiss
it. She was hurt and upset and wanted to lash out. I think
she felt like she was worthless."

"Not quite worthless," I pointed out. "Someone was
willing to pay thirty grand."

"Except that they didn't," Lydia said. "That was a

letter from the agency, saying the couple had changed
their mind. When they did, I did, too. When she read the
letter, Stacie was hysterical. It was bad enough to learn
about it that way, but she kept screamin', 'I'm not worth
anything. They didn't even want me!' I tried to tell her
that Scott wanted her, but she kept cryin' and sayin'
things about him bein' poor and that maybe they'd have
to give away their baby if they ever had one. I tell you,
she wasn't thinkin' clear."

"I don't blame her!"

"No," Lydia agreed. "That's partly what I've been
tryin' to explain. My girl ain't thinkin' clear. Scott may
think you can talk to her, get her away from Hatfield.
Maybe so. That would be wonderful. But I'm not so
sure, and my concern is for her safety."

"Quick question," I said. "Does Hatfield own dogs?"

She had recovered sufficiently to scowl at me. "What
is your fascination with dogs?"

I told her about the canine traces in the truck. Grant
hadn't said it was confidential, and this might help move
the investigation forward.

"Oh," Lydia said. It was a tiny, awful little sound.

"What?"

"I saw, in the Justia listing, that his holdings also include the Whippy Whippet Dog Obedience Schools."

I had seen their ads on late-night TV. They had one of
the worst slogans I'd ever heard, uttered by a badly ani-
mated computer-generated dog: "If you can't beat it,
whippet!" The ads mostly featured hunters and out-
doorsmen who looked like they'd beat their dogs.

"That's great," I said.

"Really?"

"No," I said. "I thought maybe I could actually rule
him out."

"Are you trying to find the killer on your own?" Lydia asked.

Lydia turned away, reached into her bag, and fished around. She emerged with a tissue. She dabbed her dry eyes—this lady was *strange*—then rose unsteadily, and I offered her my hand. My newly manicured nails made her hardened fingertips seem even sadder.

"Not as such," I said. "I'm sort of friends with the head investigator. Just lifting up rocks, seeing what's under there that might help."

"Part of me believes he is quite capable of murder, that he is a monster."

"Which part of you believes that?" I asked.

"The overly protective mother, I suppose." She pursed her lips. "Please think about what I asked before. She responds to money. That might be the hook we need to get her out of this."

She didn't say it, but my astute, paranoid ears could've sworn they heard, "Like all you people" at the end of "She responds to money." I hoped to high holy heaven I was wrong.

Lydia sniffled back hidden tears, then turned and made her lengthy exit back down the parking lot stairs. I just stood there watching her descend. She never looked back.

I got in the car and drove down the ramp, trying not to look at her as I passed. Maybe I should've offered her a lift, but I didn't want to. I was already more involved with her than I had expected, desired, or wanted to think about. The whole thing stank. My father's mistress, whom I met because someone was killed by my loading area. What good karma was hidden anywhere in that logline? On top of which, I had a deli to run and a staff in whose lives I was involved and men who had relationship *mishugas* that didn't seem to match my own meshuga needs. Why did I need to take on three more nutcases?

Because, like all the mountains in your life, they're there.

More than that, though, I had a feeling—I don't know why—that somewhere through this was the exit sign to the whole matter of Mr. Silvio and his ripped-up throat.

With rush hour long over, the ride home was even quicker than usual. Only as I got out of the car and the light came on did I see that there was a brown paper bag poking from the well with the water bottle.

I picked it up. It wasn't very heavy. I realized that Lydia must have placed it there when she went into her purse and came out with a tissue. I thought that had taken a little longer than it should have.

I felt fairly comfortable ruling out an explosive device. I unrolled the top of the bag and spilled the contents onto the seat. Out spilled a small stack of photographs and scraps of paper. I wish I could say I had a sentimental "Oh God" moment, but I didn't. I think I was probably protecting myself. I put my knees against the seat and fingered through the messy pile.

They were old images. There was a photo of young Lydia outside with baby Stacie, presumably. My father was sitting on a lawn chair in the background. The next photo was taken earlier, when Lydia was pregnant with Stacie, again presumably. One hand was on her belly, and the other was being used to shield her eyes from the flash. There was a school photograph of Stacie wearing a black blouse and black barrettes in her hair, and she was smiling. She looked to be around seven years old and was seemingly content with her young life.

After that the photos predated my half sister. They were black-and-white images of strangers, who, I could only assume, were my distant half relatives. The pictures showed the usual stuff, mustached men standing in yards in front of houses, bored and tolerant women humoring the photographer, and children thrilled by the modern advancements of film technology, their clothes nothing more than shapeless fabric with buttons.

I flipped over several of the photos, hoping they would offer up some clues as to who these people were and why Lydia wanted me to see them. Only one had writing on the back, an antique picture of a tall young man with a big cowboy hat and one of those stubby neckties that were popular in the late 1800s, his giant hands hanging at his sides, his rugged suit almost resembling Herman Munster's. The man stared deeply into the heart of the camera, the mighty sun casting deep shadows on his face from the brow down to his cheeks. In pencil, on the back, was written "Devil Anse."

Oh. Maybe the pictures weren't for me.

Well, I'm not sure how I feel about being a messenger. I didn't know if I wanted the responsibility for any of this.

Now that I thought about it, consciousness itself was no longer a responsibility I wished to bear.

I fed the cats their usual fare and looked in my fridge for mine. It was practically empty, save for half a garlic clove and some leftover Chinese food from a few nights before Joe Silvio died. I closed the fridge door and leaned both my hands and stiff arms on the kitchen counter, clicking the tip of my tongue off the inside of my bottom lip.

I'd heard about this new pizza place in Five Points and decided one more junky meal would do me good. Gathering up my second wind, I put my jacket back on and got back in the car. Ten minutes later I was sitting in front of two slices of New York–style, gooey-cheesed, grease-dripping, easily folded pizza. I didn't even do the usual napkin blot to soak up the extra grease. I sat in the booth as I blissfully chewed my giant bites. I stared out the window and gazed at nothing in particular in the foreground. Then my focus shifted to the background, where I noticed an American flag fluttering on a pole. I followed the pole down to a large brick building with a mural painted on the side depicting President Andrew Jackson with a strong-looking woman, who I was fairly certain had to be his wife, Rachel. I remembered from another Charlton Heston movie that she never lived to see him become president.

"Everything okay, miss?"

I looked up. You could tell the parlor was new, since the employees still had that ready-to-please attitude.

"Yes, thank you," I told him. "Things are much better now."

He gave me a funny look as he walked away. I realized then that he had meant the pizza, not with my life.

As I told my staff, you never know what's on customers' minds when they're sitting alone at a table, and that the rule of thumb was to approach them as gingerly as a cop coming up to a car on a routine speeding stop. It just never occurred to me that I would be one of those whack jobs on the other end of a server's greeting.

Chapter 15

When I arrived at the deli, the place smelled of fresh coffee and sizzling onions. I could hear Luke singing from the kitchen, and through it all came Dani's tinkling-bell laugh. Thom even greeted me with a big smile as she counted money into the register.

I should always arrive to work twenty minutes late, I thought, although lately I had been.

"Sorry, guys. I hit some construction traffic," I said.

"Nothing to worry about," Dani said cheerfully, though there was something a little off with her smile. "We've got it under control!"

"You okay?" I asked.

"Yo. I be fine," she said.

I wasn't convinced, but I let it go.

"How was last night, after I left?" I asked Thom.

"Everything went smooth as velvet."

"How was Mr. Reid?"

She broke a roll of quarters into the till and gave me a funny look. "As pertains to what?"

"I don't know," I lied.

"He was the short list of what every host should be,"

Thom said. "He was very gracious and gave everyone a good tip."

"What did you talk about?"

"Honey, what are *you* talking about?"

"Did you discuss the weather or the meeting—"

"Oh," Thom said knowingly . . . and wrongly. "You want to know if he said anything about running those pictures? He didn't."

"I see," I replied, improvising. "He should have apologized."

"Yesterday's news," she said, not realizing what she'd said.

"Did he say anything else?"

Thom was losing her patience. "About what? Can't you just spell it . . . oh," she said again, once more knowingly and wrongly. "You mean about how the vote is leaning."

I made a noncommittal face.

"I don't know. A.J. and Dani may have overheard, if you want to ask them. I didn't. I figure the good Lord will let you know when and what He wants you to know."

"You've probably got a point," I said.

"I know I do."

"Was he surprised I wasn't there?" I decided to be a little more aggressive.

"What? God? You askin' what God thought?"

"No," I said. "Mr. Reid."

"Girl, you were there."

"Only for a minute."

"So? I don't think he gave two thoughts to any of us, and if he did, he did not share them with me. He didn't come into the kitchen, and I'm sure if things hadn't run smooth outside the kitchen, I'd've heard from him. Now, are you writin' a book about last night, or can I finish this so we can open?"

I told her to carry on, and a minute later the front door swung open and in walked our first customers of the day. The Repeat Returners, who gave me a dirty look as A.J. went to take their order, and a young couple I thought were tourists. You can always tell by the big lenses on their cameras. Except that the male half took pictures of the kitchen. I knew why, and at this point, I didn't give two shakes. As long as they ordered something, they could take all the after-the-fact photos they wanted.

I went to the kitchen, gave a quick wave to Newt, Dani, and Luke, and headed for my office.

"Hey, you need to approve the playlist for open mic night?" Luke shouted.

"No," I called back. "As long as it's Luke unplugged."

"Always, always." He raised some fingers in a sign whose meaning completely eluded me.

I heard Dani say, "Unplugged rules!"

They made it seem so easy, so uncomplicated. Stinkin' kids.

I put my bag on the back of my chair; sat in the chair, which I suddenly, irrationally viewed as an antagonist; and thought about what I had to do. Not what I wanted to do, not what I felt obligated to do, just what I knew I needed to do.

I had to go see Stacie.

That brief glimpse of her I'd caught had stayed with me all night. She looked like I felt: lonely. That spoke to me, louder than it should have. In a way, we'd both experienced the same kind of childhood: Dad wasn't fully engaged. She was in love with someone but drawn to someone else. That wasn't an exact matchup, but I understood the kind of riptides that could cause. She felt estranged from her mother. Mine had passed, but hers had tried to sell her. Those were two sides of the same sense of loss.

There was another part of this, though, and that was, what kind of advice would I give her? I didn't know much about Scott, but I was not sure that I would've hooked my twentysomething life to his star. Childhood sweethearts or not, maybe she wanted something more. And if she didn't, was it my responsibility to try and coax her in that direction?

Why? What did ambition ever do for you? I asked myself. Wouldn't you have rather met and married a poor guy and been happy, some schlub who had a shoe shop in the East Village or ran a bar or sold back-issue magazines in a loft on Fourteenth Street?

"Why did you dump this in my lap, people?" I asked.

The chair creaked. I told it to shut up. Decided, I left the office.

I stepped out in time to see the ladies leave without tipping. A large family of eight sat down. Business was okay and the staff was moving around like a well-oiled machine that wasn't even noticing me, so I slipped out.

It was a damp day—fitting—with a misty rain. I didn't need an umbrella, just a baseball cap. I had decided to walk over to the child-care center Scott had mentioned. The not-long walk was one of those things I found myself having to force myself to do, like the time I had to go up and collect my sixth grade diploma and I felt like everyone in the world was watching me and I didn't want them to. Or when I walked down the aisle with Phil and had a feeling like I was doing something incredibly dumb, and I had to tell myself it was just nerves and force myself to think, *Left foot, right foot, left foot . . .*

The place was on Seventh, between Broadway and Church. I smoked one of my "healthy" cigarettes on the way to chase away the jitters. I didn't know why I felt them. I didn't have a dog in this fight. If we got along, great. If she listened to me, fine. If she didn't, okay. The worst thing that could happen was I'd waste some time and breath.

No, I thought. *The worst thing that can happen is she likes you and you don't like her. You'll feel obligated to see her now and then, harming yourself to keep from hurting her. Thanks, Dad. Damn you.*

As I walked, I heard a car horn toot to my left. I didn't know if it was for me, but I looked over. It was Grant flying solo in his cop car. He pulled to the curb, rolled down the window, and asked if I wanted a lift somewhere.

"I'm okay," I said.

"You want to get in, anyway?" he asked.

I said sure. Because I was either a masochist or insane. Because Luke and Dani definitely were not.

"What's doing?" I asked.

"Heading out to see Brenda Silvio," he said.

"Oh."

"The funeral is tomorrow, and she's planning to leave town immediately after and stay with friends. I wanted to talk to her. This is my shot."

"What do you expect her to say?"

He raised and lowered a shoulder. I didn't know him well, but I knew that gesture.

"You have something," I said.

"Just questions."

"What about?"

"I can't tell you," he said.

"Why?" I added angrily, before I could stop myself, "Because we're not dating anymore?"

He looked disappointed. "No, Gwen. Because I told you about the canine presence and you told a third party."

"Lydia?"

He made an "uh-huh" face.

"How did *that* come to your attention?"

"She came to the station, asked to see me, wanted to know what it would take to put someone in protective custody."

"Who?"

"Can't tell you that, either," Grant said.

"Come on. She's family. Almost."

He seemed puzzled. "How's that?"

I explained the connection. He listened without responding. Then he looked down the street. "You're going to see your half sister," he said.

I didn't answer. I was being bitchy but didn't care. He accepted that.

"Look, I just wanted to tell you that I assumed whatever I said to you was between us," he said. "I would appreciate if you would respect that confidence going forward."

"Sorry," I said. "I hadn't realized it was confidential."

"Why? Because I didn't flag it?"

"Yeah."

"I expected better from you."

"I seem to be getting that reaction a lot lately." I cracked the door. "We done?"

"If you want to be."

I looked at him. "Are we still talking about the case?"

"If you want to be."

I exhaled. The windows were fogging. He switched on the defroster. The hum had the effect of a vibrating bed inside my head. It shook my thoughts into a relaxed state.

"I was upset when I left you that message," he said.

"I was upset when I got it," I replied.

"My work has always been important to me, Gwen.

Not my job or my career, but my work. Keeping people safe, making Nashville a showplace."

"I know that," I said. "I respect it."

"Well, then, understand that it was tough for me to shoulder that aside to make room for a potential relationship. No, I take that back. For an actual relationship. I like you a lot, we have—*had*—fun, and I felt you pulling away."

"I guess I just don't have my feet under me yet down here. The deli takes time, I've got the past in my head like Scrooge's ghost, and then we have Joe Silvio." I took his hand. He didn't flinch. That was a big thing, with him being on duty. "It's a lot. I screw up when I try to juggle. I've never been very good at it. I dropped the ball on this. The Grant Daniels ball. You got bruised and rolled away. I understand. I don't blame you."

"But are you upset?" he asked.

"Of course."

"I don't mean about the relationship. I mean, do you miss me?"

How to answer that. "I have missed you."

"As in a lot or as in a little?"

"As in I would like to try again, if you would."

He smiled.

"Would you have asked me that if you hadn't happened to see me walking down the street?"

"I would have," he said. "I planned to stop by on the way back from Brenda's to chat about the sanctity of whatever I mentioned, or mention going forward, in pillowless pillow talk."

"I got that message," I said. "Loose lips sink investigations. I'm sorry. I wasn't thinking."

"I don't think it did any harm," he said. "She's got other things on her mind."

"I know."

Grant looked at me. "Gwen."

That was an odd thing for him to say, especially as an entire sentence.

"Yes, Grant?"

"I have an idea."

"What kind?"

"A potentially disastrous one," he said.

"Does it involve a second woman? Because I—"

"Maybe later in the relationship," he said.

I was kidding. I hoped he was.

"No, I was thinking that you should come with me."

Truthfully? That was a stranger idea than the other one. "Why?" I asked.

"Because   And this is between us, right?"

"My lesson has been learned."

"Jason McCoy has been making things miserable for me with the chief and with the union."

"How?"

"He's been saying crap like I shouldn't be involved with this, because you and I have a relationship, that it should be turned over to another detective, who just happens to be a family friend, the man who brought him on the force—"

"As if *that* wouldn't be a conflict of interest. That's lunatic!"

"Exactly."

"Did you explain that that's crap talk?"

"I tried," he said. "But we're dealing with cover-your-butt bureaucrats. Officer McCoy has convinced the chief that he should be there with his sister to make sure that she doesn't get treated badly, just because you and she had words."

"We had *business* words," I said. "Those aren't words. Those are negotiations."

"Gwen, you're not in New York anymore. You say

anything cross about any family member, and you've got Fort Sumter on your hands."

I guessed I should have realized that by now. Especially after Scott's book report on the Hatfields and the McCoys.

"They're also afraid because the *National* is running its own operation," Grant said.

"What does that mean?" I had a feeling, and I didn't like it.

"The publisher, Robert Reid, wants to crack this one. According to some of my street sources, he's got his staff crime reporter working with about a half dozen private investigators."

I didn't like the sound of that at all. "Any of them women?" I asked.

"Yeah, two. Why?"

"Just curious," I said. Because someone had watched me get my mani-pedi. Maybe it wasn't Stacie after all. I wished I could wipe my left cheek. That prick Robert was going to get his, even if it cost me the Best in Nashville Award I deserved. "Why is he doing all this?"

"My guess is ego. When his father ran the paper, it had a reputation for the three Cs: Courage, Clarity, and Crime Busting. Since he took over, it's become known for soft news."

"Well, yeah. Family friendly, right?" I was praying hard in my head. I hoped it wasn't showing.

"Family friendly, gay sensibility, I don't know."

I almost gagged on my saliva. "Wait. Gay? Who's gay? Robert Reid?"

"Yeah. You didn't know?"

"No." Oh, he was so going to die badly.

"Well, so much for New York savvy. I thought you

would have picked that up in the time it took you to slam and reslam your back door."

"No, I didn't," I sputtered. "I guess I'm still getting used to the difference between what is gentlemanly charm down here and what is gay."

Grant chuckled. "Didn't you see *Gone with the Wind*?"

"I did," I said.

"Rhett Butler?"

"Yeah, but I always thought Ashley Wilkes was kinda gay."

He seemed pained

My mouth was saying kind and witty words, but my brain was boiling. That son of a bitch Robert had used me. He'd lied to my face, to my left cheek, to my chewing mouth so he could get close to me and find a way to use me for information. Or at least to make sure no one else got close for an exclusive. Yeah, he would've invited me back to his place—to interview me about what it was like when I found the body. *The scumbag.*

Grant was suddenly very quiet. He flicked the wipers on and off to clear away the misty film. "So can your other business wait?" he asked.

"To tell you the truth, it can and probably should," I said. "My head's not quite in that game right now."

He looked at me with a kind of intensity I'd never seen in him. It had been a long time since I'd had car sex, and then only once. We illegally, lustfully pulled over in Central Park during a snowstorm, on a date with an orthopedic surgeon. He was about twenty years older— I guess I was looking for a replacement for my sage, gray-haired NYU prof—and just as we were wrapping it up, he jerked funny and hurt his lower back. It was in the early days of cell phoning, and he had only a pager. I had to walk to Central Park West to call for an ambulance.

Grant said, "So will you come with me to talk to Brenda?"

It took me a moment to come back from snowy New York. "Sorry? Tell me why again?"

Grant grew impatient. "Listen, Gwen. Reid with all his gumshoes and me with all my officers have come up with nothing so far. I need to know more about Joe, and the only ones who can tell me are his widow and his brother-in-law."

"Are they suspects?"

"Not even unofficially," Grant said. "Is this between us?"

"No, I'm going to tell Reid." I added as his expression darkened, "Kidding."

"Joe had a term life insurance policy that didn't pay much, and the bakery was hers before they were married and is again, so there doesn't appear to be any motive."

"Did you know that a guy named Stephen Hatfield wants to buy it?"

"Rotten guy," said Grant.

"Well, they're suing him for a variety of legal reasons."

Grant seemed impressed. "You've been doing some homework."

"I get around," I said.

"We know about that lawsuit, but Brenda and Joe were both on the same page there. No conflict. But what we just discussed is pretty much all we know about the two McCoys. The Internet is great for Lions Club archives, newspaper morgues, and finding old relatives and classmates, but it doesn't tell you much about low-profile people with a privately held company."

"You're thinking that with me there, it'll be easier to open her up?"

"Right. Jason McCoy's been itching to talk to you. Why not let him? He won't be able to watch after his sister *and* give you the third degree."

"Divide and conquer. Okay. But isn't it a little tacky, right before the funeral and all?"

"No reason you can't come to the house to pay your respects."

"Except that Officer McCoy thinks I killed his brother-in-law."

"He's an idiot," Grant said. "He's not even a good cop. He was grandfathered in—literally—because his uncle and grandfather were cops. His uncle's former partner is his guardian angel."

"Is his family still on the force?"

Grant shook his head. "His uncle started a private security firm about five, six years ago. More money in that. His grandfather is eighty-one and retired. Still does some PI work on the side."

The way he said that made me say, "Don't tell me."

"Yep. He's working for Reid. That's how we got tipped off. He's still sharp, but he tends to talk too much."

Grant tapped a Tic Tac from a container. He slipped the container back into his shirt pocket. I saw his gun in his shoulder holster. For some reason that turned me on. A man who cared about his breath and was equipped to protect me. I knew there was something primal that had appealed to me about this man.

"The good news is, Jason will behave because of his sister and because mourners will be arriving about an hour after we do," Grant said. "Hey, he never specified where and when he wants to talk to you. I'm just giving him what he wants."

A pawn in a game, I thought. The idea of being used

by another Southern gentleman brought me down a little from my high. But he was right. I forced myself to focus on the game plan. "Shouldn't we arrive separately?"

"Frankly, it helps me if we don't," he said. "I can honestly tell the chief I thought the whole thing over and decided, yeah, my brother in blue deserves his shot."

I couldn't help myself. "So I'm your little get-out-of-a-fix-free card, eh?"

"Call it penance for dog saliva," he replied.

Okay . . . I deserve that, I thought. But it struck me as a perfect description of my life so far. I wasn't the dog, I wasn't the killer, and I wasn't the dead man. Yet somehow, the bill still ended up on my plate. That wasn't self-pity talking: I was a scrapper, not a wallower. It was a fact. Other people's messes always seemed to find me— Phil's mother issues, Dad's wanderlust, my staff's romances and spats, people dying while I'm trying to work, the guy I was hot for being gay. Maybe that was a way to bond with Stacie. Commiserating over people who left their trash on our psychological stoops.

Grant was still holding my hand and gave it a little thank-you squeeze. It was worth whatever egg in the face this little undertaking would leave me with. It brought me back to the moment. For that moment, I felt content.

He pulled from the curb, and less than two minutes later we were on 65, headed north.

Chapter 16

I'd always been fond of numbers. Maybe that was because so much of my life had never added up. Parents, dating, even friends growing up. I always picked the kids who were new on the block or were shunned by the cliques. The black girl, the girl with a Jewish mother and a Muslim father—talk about issues!—the deaf boy who liked rock concerts because he could feel the music through the floor. In math, I had control. There was only one right answer.

In retrospect, thinking about how I tried to help those kids fit, remembering the single-minded zeal with which I tried to solve the Hopewell murder after he plopped into my gravy, I realized it was all to make the numbers work. There was a solution. I just had to find it.

Like now. Only this one had more variables than the last, and none of them seemed to have much to do with the dead man. Sexual hookups among the dramatis personae? Had those in Stacie and Stephen, my dad and Lydia, Robert and not me. Motive? So far, nobody that hated Joe, but there were plenty of people who might've wanted to frame me, from the neo-Nazis who once targeted my uncle Murray to the owner of the Blue

Elephant, who I knew was hurting and could certainly use the Best award. I didn't know Singh very well. Scott had said he was dating his mother, but for all I knew, he also had eight kids and a mother-in-law. Murder could be both a mercantile tactic and an emotional release. My brain even reached so far as to wonder if Scott would kill to bring Lydia out of the woodwork and get me and Stacie together. Or Robert. Would he generate a gruesome homicide to show he had the chops to cover one?

That's what I mean about variables and *The L Word* chart and numbers not seeming to tote up.

Grant must have been considering a lot of the same things as we drove. Except for the occasional crackle of the police radio and the smooth mechanical voice of the GPS, we drove in complete silence. It wasn't awkward, though. He was on duty. His brain was working. I was accustomed to that.

We approached a quiet suburban street named Webster Drive.

"There it is," he said. "The one with the gated yard."

The house was the last one on a cul-de-sac. Nothing too fancy, nothing very expensive. It was a pretty brick house with flowers on the windowsill and a three-foot iron gate. There were small round solar lights lining the slate walkway.

Grant pulled into the driveway and killed the ignition.

"You okay?" he asked.

"Surprisingly, yes."

"I won't let him manhandle you."

"I won't let him, either," I said, my can-do feminist self-reliance meeting his cool macho head-on, like two stags on the plain.

"Let's do it," he said, opening the door.

We walked up, Grant in the lead. He punched the bell with a knuckle.

Of course I heard a dog barking. Then another. Grant and I exchanged knowing looks, though he couldn't have come across as many dogs as I had since this thing started.

I heard the clack of approaching heels on hardwood floors and a woman shout, "Hitch, lay down! Macguffin, no!"

The door opened a few feet, and the strong smell of cinnamon wafted out. A woman of about forty-five with long light brown hair, full bangs, big eyes, a round face, and a cute figure stood before us. She was about five-foot-two. Without the black stilettos she would barely top five feet. She was dressed in a black button-down blouse and a skirt.

A cigarette hung from her lower lip. That would account for the rough voice I remembered.

"Mrs. Silvio?" Grant asked.

She nodded.

"Detective Grant Daniels," he said. "This is Gwen Katz."

The woman's eyes moved toward me like little machines. The rest of her face was immobile. Even the curling cigarette smoke seemed to stand still. Strangely, her eyes were not bloodshot. Either she'd cried it all out the first day or I needed to find out which brand of liquid tears she was using.

Or maybe she's one of those delayed-reaction mourners, I thought. *People who don't lose it until all their public responsibilities of grief and receiving comfort have ended.*

"Come in," she said, turning on a cloud of smoke like the Lone Ranger.

Tonto was not far off. Jason McCoy lurked behind her, by a big gold-framed hall mirror. He was not what I had imagined. He was not a big man, only about five-five, with the same big eyes and round face, but bald. He was wearing a black suit and a confused look.

We followed Brenda into her large dining room. Jason hung back to bring up the rear. The room smelled like apple pie. Brenda motioned for us to sit at the large oak table covered with pies, plates of cookies, chips and dips, and cans of soda near an ice bucket. A spread for mourners. The table leg nearest the hall was chewed up. I saw the culprits lying around it like two large fur wraps, a pair of smallish French bulldogs. I could see into the living room from where I stood. In front of the TV, on a large white sectional, sat a blond-haired gentleman— a tall man, judging by his long legs. He was watching what must have been a recording of a college basketball game, since it was so early in the day.

Brenda noticed me staring.

"That's Dave," she told us.

She said it loud enough so that Dave heard. He turned and looked at us and went back to watching the game.

"He was Joe's best friend since grade school." She fixed her big robot eyes on me. "He's taking this very hard."

"Understandably," Grant said.

Brenda slid into a chair at the head of the table. Jason closed the pocket doors between the living and dining rooms so we'd have privacy, but not before the dogs slipped in. The officer then took up a position behind his sister. I couldn't decide if he looked more like a regent to the queen or a bailiff at an arraignment. Either way, it was a wall of McCoy. I flashed to one of those amber-tinged daguerreotypes from the nineteenth century, a historical photo from the era of the Hatfield-McCoy hostilities.

Our hostess gestured to two other chairs. Grant held mine out for me. He sat beside me at the near end of the table. The dogs were between us. Every breath seemed like a little growl. I sneezed. Brenda took a final drag on her cigarette and ground it out hard. She glared at me through the smoke like a Disney villainess.

"Officer McCoy," Grant said, "Ms. Katz and I figured it was time you met. Got to ask your questions, clear the air."

I looked at Brenda. "Mrs. Silvio, I just want to tell *you* how sorry I am for your loss—"

"Words," she said, cutting me off.

I swallowed the oath that would naturally have come flying forth.

"Mrs. Silvio, Gwen is here to try and clear the air and answer any questions you both have about what happened," Grant said. "She came willingly with no preconditions."

"We appreciate that," Jason said. "We *do* have some questions."

Grant put a hand on my knee out of view of our hosts. I guess that was my signal when to speak and when to shut up. I'd defer to him on that. Following my instincts would result only in corn chips being flung.

Jason stepped from behind his sister and leaned on the table like a little, hairless Perry Mason.

"You say you didn't know my brother-in-law, even though you've been doing business with the bakery for over a decade."

"I've been down here less than a year," I said. "During that time, someone else was doing my ordering."

"Joe sometimes drove the delivery truck," Jason said.

"I almost never got in before seven," I replied. "Thomasina Jackson, my manager, is the early riser on the crew."

"You have time cards to prove that?" Jason asked.

"No."

Grant was working my knee with his hand like an ape at the controls of a space capsule. Up, down, up, down. I jerked my leg, and he stopped. I sneezed.

"So you can't prove that," Jason said.

"And you picked a fight with me," Brenda added hotly. "Why?"

"That had nothing to do with your late husband," I said. "He was trying to make good on what I admitted was our screwup. As you may recall, I appreciated it."

Jason was regarding me like I imagined he would look at a target on a shooting range. No, scratch that. Like a living, fleeing felon he felt he had a right to shoot.

"You're a single lady," he said.

"I am."

"In a strange town."

"An unfamiliar town," I said. "The Emerald City would be a strange town."

His brow scrunched for a moment. Then he gave up trying to figure that out. "We only have your word that you did not know, and were not interested in, Joe Silvio."

"That's right," I said. "And may I add, you have only your tawdry suspicions to think that I was interested in the married Mr. Silvio."

"Who happened to be co-owner of a bread factory," Jason said. "And you happen to use a *lot* of bread, almost as much as our biggest customer, the Fried Sandwich Shack. How do we know you weren't looking to woo your way into a discount?"

"Hold on," Grant said. "That's—"

"A motive!" Brenda said, cutting in.

"Ridiculous," Grant said.

"Not to someone who is worried about the bottom line!" Brenda replied.

"*Someone?*" Grant said. "What exactly do you mean, Mrs. Silvio?"

I sat there silently as Grant made ready not only to defend my honor but also to stave off what was starting to smell like an attack on my people. God, I was tired of that stereotype. What was more disappointing, though, was that by trotting it out, the wall of McCoys was adding bricks to the stereotype of Southerners as ignorant, provincial racists—which I knew was not true.

Brenda muttered something about New Yorkers, Jason ran some statistic up the flagpole about homicide and spurned lovers, and even the dogs barked. I reached out, grabbed a white-chocolate-covered pretzel, and chewed it up in a few bites. I took another and did the same. Between this and Robert's meringue and the cigarette I craved, this homicide was not going to do my health any good.

"People," I said as I chewed a third pretzel, "this is getting us nowhere."

Grant and Jason had both leaned forward like leashed tigers. Grant sat back, and Jason stood. The dogs had lifted their heads like dogs, and when order was restored, they lay back on their paws.

Grant ended the brief time-out.

"You've laid out a lot of assumptions, Officer McCoy, but no evidence," he said. "If you have anything, anything at all, a scrap of fact to present, let's have it."

Jason's spine straightened, and his head went back. His expression said, "Evidence? Who needs evidence?" His mouth said, "I don't have proof, Detective Daniels. I only know what I suspect."

"Great," Grant replied. "That and a buck will get you coffee."

Jason sneered. "Not at Starbucks." He looked at me. "We know where you been getting your cuppa."

"You're wrong," I said. "Cops drink free at Murray's."

The sneer deepened. It must've been the emphasis I put on *cops*. Or the idea that a Jew would treat anyone to anything.

Grant reached into his pocket. "Mrs. Silvio, I want you to look at something."

He got up and handed her a folded stack of papers. She set it down before her and lit another cigarette from a pack beside the ashtray.

"My phone bill," she said.

"Your home landline," Grant said. "You see the numbers marked with a yellow line?"

"You can't really miss them, can you?"

"It's a business phone," Grant said. "York's Sports Memorabilia on Fourth Avenue N."

"That's right."

"It was called fifty-six times last month, nearly twice a day, and fifty-three times the month before that." He looked around the room. "I don't see any autographed balls or game-used jerseys on the walls. Perhaps in the living room?"

Brenda blew smoke. "Those things are costly. We do not have that kind of disposable income."

"Then, what? Did either of you know the owner, a Tolliver York?"

Brenda grinned. "We did. Very well. He's sitting in the next room."

Grant seemed puzzled.

"Uses his middle name," I said. "Who wouldn't with a first name like Tolliver?"

Grant was just a half step behind me. "David, your husband's best friend."

Brenda smiled sweetly. "They talked, as you suggested, sometimes two or three times a day."

"What about?" I asked.

"I don't see how that's any of your business," Jason replied.

"What about?" Grant asked.

Jason's lips became a single, angry line.

"I didn't eavesdrop," Brenda said.

"What about when they were together?" Grant asked, pressing.

"They laughed a lot," she said with a kind of misty reflection, like a seer. "Talked about their childhood. Playing sports, chasing girls. Including me."

"They both chased you?" Grant asked.

"Those two and Chuck Gailey and Bull Griffith and a whole bunch of others. I was very popular."

"So they were like brothers?"

"Very much so," Brenda said. "I remember when Dave served in Iraq. He volunteered for the first war. Joe was very, very upset. Very worried." She smiled. "That was actually the start of his sports business. Before he left, Dave was concerned his mother would throw all his memorabilia out or sell it at a yard sale. She never really understood it and thought it was a waste of money. We took it in, stored it in the spare room. That was the time when online buying and selling were just getting started, and Joe would pick up items for Dave to surprise him with when he came back. That gave him the idea of opening the store."

"Where did the money for the shop come from?" Grant asked.

"Dave's folks," she said. "They won a million and a half dollars in the state lottery. They moved to Hawaii and gave him what was left over."

"So Joe had no interest in it."

"Only as a friend," she said.

"Mind if I talk to Dave?"

"Not at all, but I don't think you'll get much from

him," Brenda said. "He's been very, very upset. He's been comforting himself with Mr. Jack Daniels. It's an odd thing, Detective. Looking after him has helped me not focus on how upset *I* am." Jason laid a comforting hand on her shoulder. She pulled on her cigarette and exhaled. "I'm sure it will hit me at some point."

Grant took the phone list and tucked it back in his pocket. He walked to his chair and leaned on the back. The dogs growled again. Brenda silenced them.

"Who knew where your husband was going to be that morning?" he asked.

"The bakers," she said.

"You already spoke to them," Jason put in.

"Baba and Marvin," Grant said.

"That's right," Brenda said. "They adored Joe."

"So they said," Grant replied.

"He gave them season tickets to the Titans games every Christmas. He was a very thoughtful employer."

I could have sworn Jason's eyes shot to me at the word *Christmas,* but maybe I imagined it.

"Anyone else in Joe's circle?" Grant asked.

"I've already talked to everyone around here, everyone he worked with, including the farmer who sold McCoy's their eggs," Jason said.

"I read your report," Grant said.

"Then you know there's nothing wrong on this end," Jason said.

He looked at me again. Maybe it wasn't my religion or my city of origin. Maybe he just hated all women who weren't his sister. I didn't see a wedding band on his finger. For all I knew, he and Robert were an item.

"You have no children. Is that correct?" Grant asked.

"You know she doesn't," Jason said.

"Just checking," Grant said, watching Brenda's reaction.

The woman had grown distant when he asked. Obviously, that was not by choice. One of them couldn't.

"Did you ever try to adopt?" I asked.

Brenda fired a look at me. "What is that your business?"

"Did you?" Grant asked.

"How dare you both!"

"*Did* you?" Grant demanded.

"No!" she said. "We did not have time for children. Running the bakery after my father died was a full-time operation. I had a family full of policemen." She threw the side of her head in Jason's general direction. It wasn't a loving gesture. "There was no one but Joe, and he worked more hours than any man ought to."

She began sobbing. They were not crocodile tears, surprisingly. I didn't know what about this woman was real, but the tears seemed to be.

Grant stood in contemplation. "I guess that does it for now," he said. "Thank you, Mrs. Silvio. I'm sorry for your loss, and please accept my apologies for the intrusion. I hope you understand we just want to find the person or persons responsible."

"Of course," she said. She crushed her half-finished cigarette and looked at me. "Ms. Katz, may I ask you a question?"

"Certainly," I said.

I'd already risen, and Grant had stepped up beside me. I didn't need the support, but it was nice to know it was there.

"Are you always as pushy as you were when we spoke on the phone?"

"I don't see what that has to do with anything," Grant said.

"No, it's okay," I told him. "I was . . . pushy. I was stressed about my order. I had a new employee starting that day, a broken dishwasher, no repairman, and other stuff going on."

I didn't have to look at Grant to know that he knew that I meant him.

"Was it also that time of month?" Jason asked.

"Officer, are you out of your mind?" Grant wailed.

"We are permitted to ask that question," Jason said.

"No, it is a question that is permitted during a psych evaluation when a doctor has already determined that a female suspect has a hormonal imbalance," Grant said. "Not a single one of those requirements applies."

Jason took the rebuke without flinching and without withdrawing the question. Which I didn't bother answering.

I looked back at Brenda. "Even for us New Yorkers, most of us, anyway, there's a big gap between being hostile—sorry, *pushy*—and homicidal. Most of us don't cross that line."

"Most, but not all," Jason insisted.

"No, not all. But if you check my record, and I'm willing to bet you have, you'll find that I have never been arrested, I was never the cause of domestic violence, and I have never, in fact, even received so much as a parking violation. Or, for that matter, even a health code violation. If you check TSA records, you will discover that it has never even been necessary to pat me down at an airport. I am a rational woman, Mrs. Silvio, Officer McCoy, even when I am under pressure or PMSing or being harassed by police or hounded by a public that wants to have a peek inside my house of horrors."

Brenda averted her eyes.

"I'm sorry, Mrs. Silvio, but you asked. Yes, I have been tense. But not tense enough to kill anyone." *Except Robert Reid,* I thought.

"Your business has picked up since this happened, has it not?" Jason asked.

"Yeah," I said, picking up a little steam, "it has. And, gee, who among my people wouldn't revel in that? Oh, wait. *Me.* I'd trade all of this week's receipts for one day of normalcy, Officer McCoy. One day where all of you would back off."

"It's all right," Grant said, putting an arm around me.

I shook it off. "It isn't all right. Even if I had something to hide, even if I were a serial killer, we are innocent until proven otherwise—"

"Gwen—"

I went on. "You're upset. It's a shock. Hey, we all have tsuris. We all have *troubles*. That doesn't give you an excuse to open a can of bias and start flinging accusations."

"You were the only one at the scene!" Jason yelled back.

"Except for the killer!" I shouted. The dogs started barking. I wanted to kick them. "I didn't know Joe Silvio! He was there on time with my order! I don't even have a goddamn dog!" And as if to punctuate my outburst, I sneezed three times in a row.

Brenda came over to calm the dogs as Grant led me from the dining room. He slid a pocket door closed behind us as the dogs whammed against it.

"Gwen, calm down."

I was shaking. I started to cry. The days had piled up, and I finally gave in under the weight. He ushered me out to the car, helped me in, jumped around to the driver's side, and gave me his handkerchief.

I looked up, saw Brenda looking out the dining room

window. There was a glare on the glass; I couldn't tell if she was smiling or horrified.

"That went well," I blubbered.

"Actually, it went fine," Grant said. "Some things got aired, and you've pretty much sidelined McCoy. What about *you?*"

"I'll be okay," I assured Grant. He was hovering attentively across the gearshift.

"I know," he said.

"I guess that was a little pushy," I said.

"A little."

I laughed. "That guy is a redneck *putz*."

"Globalization and the world is a village notwithstanding, we still have a view of those."

I wiped my eyes, blew my nose, and clutched the handkerchief. It was silly, but right now that was a source of strength. His, something a man had given me.

"I'm sorry I brought you," Grant said.

"Don't be. I needed that."

"Why don't we get some coffee, the over-a-dollar kind, before I take you back?"

"I have a better idea," I said. "Why don't you take me to the offices of the *National*?"

"Why? What's there?"

I said, "The Second Battle of Bull Run."

Chapter 17

The *Nashville National* was located in a white brick building on Twelfth Avenue South. The office had been there since the 1930s, when the editorial and printing operations were consolidated. There were still flatbeds with big rolls of paper outside. It reminded me of what Times Square used to be like when the *New York Times* still printed its editions in midtown.

Get your head out of the past, I yelled at myself. *You hated that time, when Professor Levey used and discarded you.*

Nostalgia is the art of forgetting the bad stuff and remembering the good. It's like the eighties, which weren't just Adam Ant and Spandau Ballet. They were also Edwin Meese and censorship, movies like *Kramer vs. Kramer* winning Oscars, and tension at home.

"I really think this is a terrible idea," Grant said as we pulled up.

"Wouldn't be my first," I said. "Probably won't be my last."

There was a fine rain now, which fit my mood.

"At least let me go in with you, then," he said.

"Nah. I can handle this."

"Without violence?"

I gave him a look. "Didn't you hear what I told Officer McCoy and his sister back there? Not all of us are homicidal."

"I didn't say you'd *kill* him," Grant pointed out.

"I won't touch him, I promise," I said. I gave Grant a peck on the lips. "I'll be fine." I handed him his handkerchief.

"You can keep that," he said. "I've got an umbrella in the trunk if you—"

"I'll call a cab if it's raining," I assured him. "Now go. Catch a killer."

I pecked him again and got out. I scurried through the glass doors, past an older security guard, and told the receptionist I'd like to see Robert Reid.

"Is he expecting you?" the young man asked.

"I should think so," I replied sweetly. "The bastard's been having me watched."

Five minutes and an elevator ride to the third floor later, I was in Robert Reid's office. He was not there, his secretary informing me that he was downstairs at the loading dock. She asked if I wanted a beverage. I asked for a scotch. She asked if I was serious. I said, "No," then added, "Not yet, anyway."

It was pretty much what I'd expected. A decent view of the city; framed front pages; photos with local, state, and national dignitaries, including one president. *The one who supported gay marriage,* I thought bitterly—not because I had anything against gays or their domestic bliss, but because this gay man had not bothered to tell me he was a gay man when I thought he was courting me. That was the kind of boondoggle that turned a rainbow to sleet, even among us mostly liberal New York Jews.

There were framed pictures of Robert's beloved rottweiler on the desk and a stack of manila file folders, the top one of which was marked JOE SILVIO. I did not touch it. Maybe he was watching from behind a peephole to see if I would.

Robert strode in, dressed in a white suit, like he was the president of the Tom Wolfe fan club. He had shut the door behind him, and his expression told me he knew something was up. I figured my comment had been repeated by the receptionist. He looked a little guarded as he walked behind his glass-top desk—for protection?— but he was too hungry a newspaperman to turn me away.

"Good morning, Gwen," he said. He gestured toward a black leather chair. "Care to sit?"

"Up yours," I replied.

"I see," he said.

"I don't think you do," I told him.

He remained standing. "May I explain?"

"You may," I said, "after you answer a question."

"Shoot," he said, then chuckled nervously, eyed my purse, and added, "I mean, go ahead."

"Are you gay?"

That obviously wasn't the question he was expecting. His body relaxed slightly, as though he was at least on familiar territory.

"I am," he said. "Why?"

"No reason. Except that after our meringuey little liaison in your kitchen and our candlelit dinner I sort of thought you were interested in me. As a woman."

"I am," he said.

"You know what I mean."

"I do," he admitted, "and that's a fair complaint. I guess . . . I don't know. I suppose I was trying to be supportive."

I gave him an "Oh, please!" look. "By kissing my cheek?"

"Why not?"

"Because you knew how I would take it. You knew how I *took* it, yet you did nothing to correct my misconception."

"Fair enough," he said. "Who told you? Your cop friend?"

"Yeah," I replied. "And not because he suspected I might be interested in you. His mind doesn't run toward jealousy."

"How nice for him."

"Don't do that," I warned. "Don't go after him because he's confident."

"Confident? What's that got to do with—"

"You? And your sudden need to do a big crime story?"

His mouth twisted wryly. "Who did he talk to? Old man McCoy?"

I didn't answer.

"It doesn't matter," Robert said. "It's true. Mind you, what I told you about the *National* is also true. I want us to be family friendly, to promote the best in Nashville. But—and maybe you'll understand this better than most, given your own family background—but parental legacies can be a bitch."

"How do you know about my family background?" I asked. "We didn't talk about it that much."

"You think you're the only one who knew about your dad and Lydia, about Stacie?"

"I asked *how*," I said.

"Nothing sneaky about that. Our society writer buys shoes from her. Lydia talks. A lot."

"What about me?" I asked. "Did I not talk enough? Is that why you had me followed?"

"I put that tail on you for just one reason," Robert said. "Cross my heart and hope to get an ink stain. I wanted to know if and when you talked to the press.

Astrid had instructions to interfere if that happened. If and when you talked, I wanted it to be to the *National*."

"You could have just told me that," I said.

"The police have rules and protocols to follow. They need warrants. I don't. If it's any consolation, I've had everyone looked into."

"Good for you. It isn't." Then I came around. "Who?"

"Brenda Silvio, Jason McCoy, the bakers, even Candy Sommerton. That gal hasn't had a big story since her implants were new. Oh, and your little friend Scott Ferguson."

"What about him?"

"He used to drive for McCoy's. They caught him diddlin' your half sister in the truck while he was supposed to be making a delivery. Fired his ass on the spot."

"What about Stephen Hatfield?" I asked.

"Stacie's inamorato? Yes, him too. The families have a history."

"I heard."

"There's nothing to suggest he was anywhere near your deli that morning, though, of course, it's possible he could have hired someone. Assuming he had a reason."

"The lawsuit?"

"He had nothing to gain. The Silvios would have lost that one, it would have cost them a bundle doing so, they would have been responsible for his legal fees, and he would have been in a better position to offer them a stack of cash to get what he wanted from them in the first place."

"What about you?" I asked.

That caught him with his guard down. "What about me?"

"You mentioned Candy Sommerton. She needed a big story. Probably not enough to kill for, but who knows? You wanted a crime story, too. Maybe *you* wanted it that bad."

"It's possible," he admitted, "but then why would I be going through the motions of researching all these people? It's a pretty expensive proposition."

"Made up for with a bump in sales. You said so yourself."

"True," he said. "But eventually the killer will be found. How would it benefit me if I was he?"

"Who says the culprit will be found? You could milk this for years, every anniversary, like Jack the Ripper. Maybe cut a few more throats to give it legs."

He smiled a crooked smile. "You *are* devious. I like it."

"You would." I looked down at the stack of folders. "Mind if I see the file on Brenda Silvio?"

He fingered through the tabbed folders, found it, pulled it out. He held it to his chest like a winning poker hand. "I'll let you have it if you tell me why."

"I'm curious," I said. "I finally met her. She didn't like me, and I didn't like her."

"You met her . . . when?"

"Just now. At their house. I was with Grant."

His face went smooth as his mouth opened. "Bless you, Gwen Katz. I'll give you credit for guts."

"I'm from New York." I took the folder from his suddenly limp fingers. "I'm surprised you didn't know where I was."

"I knew you were with Grant but not where you were going," he said. "Your move caught Astrid by surprise."

"Glad to hear it," I said as I flipped through the file. It was nice to hold something tangible instead of reading something online.

There were tax records, the same phone records Grant had, time sheets showing where she was during the last forty-eight hours—just the house and the

Dumas Funeral Home, not surprisingly—and also old *National* clippings about the bakery and about her appearances at civic functions.

There was one clipping that stopped me.

Robert noticed. He had been watching me carefully. "What is it?"

"This picture," I said. "Notice anything?"

The photo was of Joe and Brenda on their wedding day. It looked like they had just had the "kissed the bride" moment and were holding hands as they began to make their final exit down the aisle.

"Not really," he said. "What am I looking for?"

I laid the folder flat on the desk, brought over a magnifying glass on a stand.

"I'm still a little at sea here," he said.

I pointed to a face off to the side. "See this man?"

"The best man?"

"Right. His name is Tolliver David York."

"The memorabilia dealer."

"Uh-huh. Childhood friend of the deceased."

"How do you know that?"

"He was at the Silvio home," I said. "Consoling the widow. Drowning his grief in a basketball game."

"Really?"

"And truly. What does he look like to you in this photo?"

Robert bent a little closer. "He looks like he's losing his best friend. But that's not uncommon in marriages. Three's a crowd."

"I know. So what if the frown is not for Joe?"

Robert straightened. "Interesting."

"Brenda said that both men courted her way back when."

"How seriously?"

"I don't know," I told him. "She kind of threw it off,

but . . . I don't know. It could be nothing. Or it could be something."

"An affair?"

It wouldn't exactly be out of place with this crowd, I thought. "Worth looking into," I suggested. I put the clipping down and tugged the edge of the phone list. "There're lots of calls to Dave's phone here. She *said* they were all from Joe."

"An affair," he repeated thoughtfully. "A murder of long-simmering passion?"

"But maybe not his passion," I said. "Could be Brenda had enough. Couples who work together either have a great relationship or a miserable one. "

"That *would* be a story," he said. He looked at me with admiration. "You're good."

"I like numbers," I said. While Robert tried to make sense of that, I said, "So how did the committee meeting go last night?"

"Fine," he said. "Your people did a tremendous job."

"I know. I was there."

"I know. I saw you."

I looked at him. "You could have said hello."

"I wasn't sure you wanted to hear it. All you offered me was a view of your ass."

"Obviously, not a part that held any appeal."

"Rebuke away," he said. "I don't blame you."

If this were an old movie, I would have slapped him. But if this were an old movie, he would have been Cary Grant, not Robert Reid, and he wouldn't have been openly gay, just egregiously ambitious. And we'd fall in love in the end, which was not how this story was going to end. So his face was spared.

"You'll be giving Astrid a different assignment?" I asked.

"She'll begin looking into that little triangle as soon as you leave."

"You'll destroy my file?"

He hesitated. Then with one swift gesture he pulled it out and handed it to me.

"Anything in here I should know?" I asked.

"Souvenir photos of you and Grant in his car."

I tore the thin folder in half, then tore each half in half separately. I threw the pieces up with both hands and watched him while they settled on his white shag rug.

"I believe we understand each other," I said.

"Completely."

"Oh, and if you hold it against me in the Best voting, I will come back and smack you."

"We're like the Antoinette Perry Awards," he assured me. "The Tony is not a measure of one's personal popularity or lack thereof."

I looked out the window, saw it was still raining. "Would you call me a cab?"

"Immediately," he said.

I started to go.

"Gwen?" he said.

I half turned.

"Do you forgive me?"

"Not yet."

"Okay," he said.

I continued toward the door.

"Gwen?"

I stopped but didn't turn.

"Would you consider, possibly, remotely, in the interest of history, giving me a one-on-one for the paper when this is over? It'll be great for—"

I was out the door and slammed it, turning *business* into just a jumble of letters.

Chapter 18

I checked in with Thom during the cab ride, which, I was pleased but not overly surprised to see, was prepaid. All I had to do was sign a voucher.

"We're fine," Thom said. "As usual."

There was not exactly a tacit criticism in her voice, just a stoic heroism.

"I'm sorry," I said. "I ran into Grant, and we got to talking."

"I'm glad to hear that," she said. "You need someone outside here, and if it was up to me, you wouldn't even *be* here for a while, after what you saw."

"Be that as it may—"

"It ain't *may,* Gwen, honey. It's fact."

"Okay. I'll still be back soon. I have one more stop to make."

"You'll be back when you're back. I gotta go."

"Dani doing all right?"

"Dani is doin' fine, considerin' she went to Luke's soiree after the Reid party last night and let on that she's a little hungover."

"I thought she seemed a little off," I remarked.

"I suspect she has hidden such things before," Thom

said. "I only found out when I saw her chuggin' OJ with a side of pickles."

I made a face. "Let me guess. Online remedies?"

"Separate ones, but she went for the double dose."

"Gotta love her."

"Or somethin'," Thom said noncommittally. Drinking and her religious beliefs did not go well together. "Got lunch crowd startin' in. Goin' now, hon."

Thom hung up. We were a block from our destination. I felt as though I could use a few drinks myself.

It was nearly noon. The light but steady rain had emptied the streets of their usual Monday morning foot traffic. I had no idea when Stacie took lunch. I wasn't even sure I wanted to talk to her. But I did want to see her, just lay eyes on her. Maybe it was a way to get in touch with a part of my father I'd never known.

A sucky part, I thought, *but even bad news is information.* The torn-up feelings I had for him needed a push one way or the other.

The cab stopped in front of Blinn Day Care. I got out and stood under the awning of the pet shop next door. I looked through the window.

There were cribs, floor mats, plastic and rubber toys, and Sammi Blinn, a very attractive and sweet young woman I knew from chats at the deli. Then there was a younger woman tending to a crying little girl. The woman was taller than Lydia, about five-eight, but had her strong cheekbones and graceful movements. When she happened to look up, I saw that she also had her mother's eyes. Her long brown hair was worn in a ponytail. There was a small engagement ring on her left hand and a tattoo on her bare right arm. It looked like a football. It was pretty low on her arm, well below the biceps. If I used a tape measure, I'd probably find it was in the exact center.

A sweet tribute to the football career of her affianced.

I waited there, admiring the gentle way she handled the kids. I couldn't imagine the things she felt when she did that. Remembering Thomasina? Imagining a time when she would have her own kids? Wanting them to have a life of comfort and attention, not like the life she had—not the life that Scott Ferguson could offer?

Maybe she doesn't really think about any of that, I thought. *I have a decade on her and New York jadedness on top of that. Maybe her thoughts are more innocent, purer.*

It occurred to me then that meeting her, I might actually poison the poor thing with something worse than she already had.

I had just about made up my mind to go when she looked up, happened to see me, and snapped her gaze back after it had already passed. She put the girl in front of a music box of some kind, went over to Sammi, said a few words, and pulled a slicker from the coatrack. I'd been made. There was no sneaking off now.

She came out the door, the bell tingling, and stepped under the awning. It was like looking into the face of Lydia before life and probably some long swims through a bottle had beaten the hell out of her.

"Gwen," she said rather than asked.

"Hi," I said.

We looked at each other—just looked. I couldn't read what she was thinking. I was aware of my heart beating a little faster, driven by uncertainty and a little fear. I was about to say something, anything—I had no idea what would come out—when she put her arms around me and hugged me tighter than I could ever remember being held. It was a grip of desperation. Not self-pity. She didn't cry, didn't clutch. She just held. As though cementing, in tangible form, the unspoken thing we shared.

Her ear was near mine. "Had lunch yet?" I asked.

"Why? Do you know a place?"

That made me laugh. She laughed. She stepped back, looked in my face, and we both laughed a little, then cried, then hugged again like long-lost sisters.

"Shit," she said.

It wasn't much, but it said a lot.

She said she'd be right back and ran into the day-care center. I peeked. I saw Sammi nod. I didn't want this to be traumatic for Stacie *and* get her fired. She came back out, took my arm, and said through a big smile, "So where's this place?"

Actually, it was a dark tavern down the street called the Bar Bar. It said only Bar, but it was written on a musical bar. It was pretty much a nightspot, but it was open for lunch. We took a booth in the back. We both ordered an iced tea.

"Not too weird," she said in a strong, sweetly accented voice.

"This, or the fact that we both ordered the same drink?"

"Both, I guess," she said. Then added another "Shit" for good measure.

"Yeah, I know."

What do you say to a sibling you've never met, who you didn't even know existed until a few days before?

"So . . . how's life?" I asked.

She laughed again, I laughed again, but this time she stopped short of crying. Our drinks arrived, and we didn't bother looking at the menu. She ordered a lunch salad. I ordered a hamburger.

"Not big on healthy eatin'?" she asked.

"Tough to do where I work."

"I eat a lot of salads 'cause that's what Thomasina fed me growin' up."

"Eat your greens," I said. "Her own kids told me she said that to them all the time."

"Would it get her in trouble if I told you I see her now and then?"

"Not at all," I said. "I don't blame you."

Stacie laughed. "She still tells me to eat greens, and she still makes me pray. Did you ever pray with her?"

"Not willingly," I said.

"You should. It helps."

I still couldn't believe Thom had kept this from me. But the kind of love she gave to this girl made it impossible to be upset.

Stacie's mood sobered. "My mother came to see you."

"Yes."

"Scott too."

"Scott too."

"I'm sorry," she said.

I reached across the table and took her hand. "Don't be. They brought me to you."

She smiled tightly.

"What can I do for you?" I asked.

She sighed and absently stirred her iced tea with a straw. "I wish I knew." The tears returned, just a few. It was sadness, not histrionics. "I'm angry at Mom. You know about the adoption?"

"Yes."

"I know I shouldn't blame her, she said she only wanted what was best for me, but it's no fun to find out your mother wanted to *sell* you."

"People do things when they're confused," I said. "Sometimes not the smartest things."

She laughed humorlessly. "That's almost what Scott said to me last night."

"Why?"

"He knows I've been seeing this guy. . . . It's a stupid thing, doesn't really mean anything, but he's real generous."

"He gives you money?"

She nodded.

"Why?"

"'Cause he knows I need it," she said.

"Do you   "

"Have sex with him? Yeah. But it's not like it sounds. I was doin' that before he started givin' me a hundred here and there."

"You said it doesn't really mean anything—"

"That's true. When I'm with him, in his big ole house, in a bed with silk sheets, I feel good about myself. The money is just somethin' extra. I keep it in a box in the bank. And when it's done one day, when one of us is tired of the other, then it's done. At least I'll have had that feelin' of bein' a queen."

"What about Scott?"

She looked off, as though she were seeing his face in the distance. "Scott . . . is like a whole other world. He's the guy I watch Jason Statham with. He's the guy who brings home *pakoras* and naan. You ever feel that way about a guy, that he's mostly a good buddy?"

"Sort of," I told her. "I've got a little of that going on right now."

"It's not a bad thing, is it? A friend you have sex with."

"Not bad," I agreed. "Though it'd be nicer if I loved the guy."

"Oh, I guess I love Scott. But Stephen is like this king. I don't love him, but he's handsome and he sure rocks my chair. You ever have *that*?"

"I did, and frankly, I would argue against it."

"Against a man boy toy?"

"No, against . . . God, I'm not even sure what to call it."

"What happened?"

"When I was your age, I was dating a professor who was way older than me. I felt special when I was with him, like I was smart enough for this genius PhD to hang around with. Even if it was just for sex."

"And then you'd go back to your real world, right?"

"Right."

"Like the other one didn't truly exist."

"Pretty much."

"Which is what I do," Stacie said.

"Except what happened after that ended was I kept trying to find it again. I kept failing. I tried to go cold turkey by marrying someone my own age. He was a jerk. When that ended, I realized I hadn't really dealt with the issues that made me want the professor in the first place."

"What issues?"

"Not feeling good about myself, not feeling smart enough."

"But you went to *college!*"

"Where I worked my ass off. I became an accountant. And do you want to know what I learned in the time I've been down here, running a restaurant? That I could've been anything. Anything! I picked this up easily. I'll bet if it had been a baseball team or a movie studio, I could've kicked that ass, too! That's what I needed to feel good and smart enough."

Stacie was thoughtful as our food arrived. My mouth was dry and my throat was raw from all the talking and yelling I'd done. I drank half my iced tea.

"You're lucky you had those experiences," she said. "You got that knowledge."

"Stacie, the knowledge I got was that I didn't know anything about myself." I waited. "And then there were the other issues that sent me looking for a professor in the first place. The father issues."

Stacie's pensive mood went black again.

"We don't have to talk about that," I said.

"No, I want to," she told me. "I think we probably got a lot of the same scars."

"I'm sure. The question is, do I let them heal and forget about them, or do we keep staring at them and picking at them?"

"You just said we've gotta understand things. I don't see how you can do that without thinkin' about 'em."

"It depends on *how* we think about them. I'm mad about what Dad did to our mothers." It sounded strange to say "Dad" in the collective, probably as strange as it was for her to hear it. But it was also nice. "The man was selfish, and that brings out our righteous indignation as women."

She laughed, but I wasn't sure she understood that.

"What I mean is, I loved him, but even when he was alive, I was angry about how he lived his life. And I'm coming to realize that what I've been doing is beating up the men around me because I'm mad at our old man."

"Don't men ever do things that deserve a beatin' on their own?"

"Yes, they do." I laughed.

"Scott sure does."

"I'm talking about the anger and disappointment that's inside me. I haven't learned to let that go, though I'm trying. I don't want to see *you* hold on to it for another ten years. It takes a lot of energy and brainpower."

Stacie considered that. "It all makes some sense, but I still like satin sheets, and I know that Scott is never going to be able to provide them."

"Then provide them for yourself," I said. "Find a way."

I was starving and took a bite of my hamburger.

Stacie forked a tomato into her mouth. She was thinking hard, she was hurting, and I just wanted to protect her from the world and all the misery it had to offer.

"So what do I do?" she said. "I truly do not know."

"Right now? I'd suggest you stop keeping things inside. Talk about them."

"Everything?"

"Every last thing, yes."

She looked at her watch, ate some cucumber, shook her head. "Scott won't like that, my mother will hate it, and Stephen will throw me out."

"You'll always have a place to go," I told her.

She gave me a look that morphed from frustration to one of the most profound thanksgiving I had ever seen. Whatever happened in my life going forward, it would be tough to top that.

"Do you know what I'm going to do?"

"No. What?" I said.

"As soon as I get back to work, I am going to call Thomasina and thank her. I'm going to thank her and tell her that she was right."

"About . . . ?"

"Prayer. It really does work."

I thought it would be tough to top what she'd said before, but obviously, it wasn't impossible.

Stacie just did it.

Chapter 19

My voice was shot, but my day wasn't done.

I went back to the deli to do *some* work, at least, spotting Thom after the lunch rush so she could get a break. Whatever the murder had done to me personally—and also to Joe—it had drawn customers. The staff was either energized or dragging, depending on who it was. Dani seemed to have recovered from her hangover: she was one of the perky ones. So was Luke. So was A.J. Two. Raylene, Newt on the grill, and Thom were shot.

I didn't tell Thom where I'd been. Maybe she'd guessed. She had a beatific look about her, as if she'd been praying between money changing, offering silent words to God for my safe conduct. Or hers, depending on how she thought I might react.

How had I reacted? It wasn't like a symphony of emotions. It was more like grand opera, complete with intermissions, curtain calls, and themes, most of which I couldn't recall. But I remembered the big one: my half sister needed me, and I had offered to help her.

After I'd paid for our lunch, I'd walked her back to Blinn's, where she gave me a full body hug that was all warmth this time. Warmth and gratitude. I wished there was someone I could tell, with whom I could share what I felt. It was then I realized that what I had said was true: it was not enough to have a lover or a buddy. You needed both.

The afternoon was slow until about three o'clock, when a small entourage arrived. They were three men and a woman, all well dressed, clearly not tourists, though I didn't recognize a single one of them. I looked at Thom, who was handing them menus; she shrugged.

Dani waited on the table. One of the men kept looking at me. He was about forty, with slicked-back black hair, smoldering eyes, and a square jaw. His suit was not off the rack at Marshalls.

I didn't really pay them any attention until they were leaving. The man who had noticed me paid the bill. He was a big man, six-three, with the kind of confidence that made women look over their shoulders and men insecure.

"Would you be Gwen Katz?" he asked. His voice had the slight sound of Appalachia: the natural slur from genetically passed-down moonshine combined with the informality of the mountain folk. He sounded like a hillbilly Dean Martin.

"I am she," I said.

I realized who he was a moment before he said it. "I am Stephen Hatfield."

He didn't make me swoon; he made me frightened. The man didn't look like a gangster; he looked like a successful businessman who fancied himself a fashion model. Yet there was something about him that made me uneasy. The shoulders? There was something about those shoulders that reminded me of a puma on its haunches, not that I'd ever seen a puma.

"Hello," I replied. I had intended to add his name to the greeting, but it stuck in my gullet.

"Is there somewhere we can talk privately?"

"About?"

He repeated the question with his insistent silence. I looked around the nearly empty dining room. "How about the corner table?"

He rotated his shoulders in that direction; his stiff neck took his head with it. "That's fine."

"Thom!" I said, motioning her over.

The other three members of the party had gone outside. They were waiting by a black limousine. If I'd seen that first, I might have figured out who he was and what was probably coming.

I asked A.J. Two to bring me a Diet Coke as we made our way to the table. I went to sit. He held my chair for me. *A gentleman mountain lion*, thought I.

He sat after I had, sweeping his knee-length black coat under him. He checked his cell phone messages while A.J. Two brought my drink. She gave me a worried little look. My look back told her it was okay. I hoped it was.

He looked around. "So this is where Joe Silvio met his maker."

"Well, not in here, exactly."

"He was a decent man," Hatfield said. "Not a proper way for a man to die."

That surprised me. I didn't expect him to spit on the man's grave, when he had one, but he was still kin to the McCoys.

Hatfield set the Sprint Evo in front of me. "Read this, if you please."

I looked at the cell phone screen. There was a text from Stacie. It was dated today, sent a few minutes after I'd left her.

I wld like 2 talk 2 u 2night abt us. I think I need 2 end it. I saw my new sister today. I have 2 chng my life. xo

You are, I believe, Stacie's *new* sister," Hatfield said.

"We each just discovered we exist, if that's what you mean."

"That is exactly what I mean. May I ask what you told her?"

"Isn't that between me and Stacie?" I asked, sounding bolder than I felt.

"It would be, and I would respect that, if it did not involve me," he said. "I will make this simple. Did you tell her not to see me anymore?"

"I did not," I assured him. "What I told her was that whether it was you or Scott or her mother, she should say what's on her mind."

"Speak up for herself, you mean."

"Exactly."

"Be an independent woman."

"That would misrepresent my advice," I said. *Misrepresent my advice? Who am I? Mr. Spock?*

"Perhaps you can clarify it for me," Hatfield said with a smile. He was now a puma who had spotted a hare. "Please," he added insincerely, a bone throw to my obvious reluctance.

"I told her not to keep things inside. I told her to trust the people close to her. If they cared about her, they would listen."

He nodded. "I go along with that. After all, it's how I conduct myself."

I had felt a moment of relief followed by apprehension. If I were parsing those sentences, I'd have said, "Good start. Now duck."

"The problem I have with that, as it pertains to Stacie, is she's a *spectacular* lay," Hatfield said. "Best I ever had. And way too fine for that busboy *jerk* she's engaged to." He said that last part loud enough for everyone to hear. "So here's my honest, from-the-heart question to you, new sister. Who's going to take her place?"

He lost me at *spectacular lay* and made me angrier with every new word he said. He could have been Michael Corleone at that moment, and it wouldn't have mattered.

"I'm sure you can find some suitable piece of ass," I said. "Might have to pay a little more, but what's a couple hundred bucks to Stephen Hatfield?"

I expected him to slap me. I didn't expect him to laugh and slap the table.

"That's rich!" he said. "I'll tell you what, Gwen Katz. I'm going to continue to take your advice and speak my heart." The laughter stopped. "I do not pay for sex. I do not lie with prostitutes. I bring a girl into my home and treat her like no one has ever treated her or ever will. That is part of what makes them so good in bed. Their gratitude." He looked around at the staff, who were standing behind the counter, like it was standing room at a hit show. "That one over there," he said. "The one with the nose and lip rings."

Dani was standing at the end of the counter, Luke to her right. They switched places like she'd been castled.

"You want to be my new girlfriend?" he asked. "Spend nights with me in my mansion, drink fine wine instead of Manischewitz?"

Dammit, was it me, or was everyone down here a closet anti-Semite?

Hatfield regarded me suddenly, as though my thoughts had penetrated his thick skull. "I'm sorry," he said. "That was a comment about quality, not any kind of ethnic disrespect."

"I'm comforted, considering all the bullshit you just said about women."

"Is it bullshit, Gwen? I've been with Stacie about six

months. Never forced her to come. Never threatened her. Before that I was with Sammi Blinn for a year."

He could not miss my surprise.

"Does that shock you? Proper, child-loving Sammi holing up with me for sex?"

"It's none of my business," I said.

He touched his nose. "Bull's-eye, Gwen Katz! That's none of your business. Just like this is none of your business. Just like if I decide to invite that little blonde behind the counter up to my place for Iranian caviar, that, too, is none of your business!"

It happened so fast that no one could stop him. Luke ran from behind the counter with a stainless-steel soup ladle. He crossed the dining room with the kitchen implement raised high and a cry of outrage rising even higher. All I could do was get up and put myself between him and his intended victim. I took the bowl of the ladle square on the bean, seeing red as I fell forward across Stephen Hatfield. By that time Thomasina had come from behind the counter, along with the only patron who had remained after Hatfield started shouting, our mail carrier, Nicolette.

They wrested Luke back as Dani ran over and got between him and me. But her eyes never left Hatfield, as though she were afraid he would grab her tiny frame and run her off to the Lonely Mountain.

Instead, Hatfield stood and lifted me gently and sat me in a chair and gave me some of my untouched Diet Coke. He was very gentle about it, very attentive.

"I'm all right," I said, gently pushing his sleeve from my face.

"Are you certain?"

"Very."

He stepped back. It was then that I noticed his entourage standing in the open door of the deli, ready to jump in if necessary.

"I am sorry I've upset some of your staff," Hatfield said.

"They'll survive."

I could hear Luke shouting in the kitchen and Thom shouting right back. They fell quiet a moment later.

"You see, Gwen, words, even honest words—or maybe *especially* honest words—have consequences. I will reply to this text that there is no reason for Stacie to trouble herself with another visit. I will tell her I do not wish to see her anymore." He leaned close and said in a whisper, "You may not realize this, but I gave her stability. I gave her dignity. We will see how long she survives with Mr. Scott Ferguson."

"Dignity . . . on her back?"

He stood, smiling again. "Your comments reveal more about yourself, Gwen, than they do about Stacie."

"You don't know anything about me."

"There you are wrong," he said. "I know that sex is not the sheer joy for you that it is for so many women. It comes with riders and codicils." He touched my face as he walked away. "A waste."

I shuddered, but not with fear. It was worse. It was excitement.

Hatfield had made a point of putting his personal card under my hand. I crushed it slowly as he walked off. He looked around as he rejoined his companions. "I beg all of your pardons for disrupting the afternoon. We will return when things have settled somewhat." He looked back at Thomasina. "The potato pancakes were very, very good."

Thom stood still and tall, like a statue of herself.

Not Dani. The young woman leaned forward and snarled, "They're latkes," just before the door closed.

Hearing her little voice, proud and assured, I actually felt tears fill my eyes.

Score one for our side—for our *sides*. The women, the Jews, and the kids who loved each other enough to risk a beating.

Chapter 20

I called Grant and left a message that whatever he was doing, wherever he was, whoever was killed between now and then, he needed to come by the house tonight.

I made sure the staff was okay before I checked to see what damage might have been done to my skull. Fortunately, I had decided I liked the scarf look, and had kept one on. That had cushioned the blow somewhat.

Luke could not have been more apologetic, and I could not assure him enough that not only was it okay, but I was also proud of him.

"Even though I don't know how the dishes would've gotten clean if you'd been arrested for assault," I told him.

He hadn't even considered that, he said. I believed him. More words that I never thought I'd think came into my head: I envied Dani.

Thom was a little rattled—the first time I'd ever seen that—because she immediately saw Luke in jail, me in the emergency room, and Dani with her legs parted at Casa Hatfield, not that she thought Dani would go willingly. But once she heard the name Stephen Hatfield, she knew things were going to get ugly.

"He's like that Mr. Potter in the James Stewart movie *It's a Wonderful Life,*" she said.

It was unusual to hear Thom make a movie reference since she rarely watched TV, with its sinful men and loose women. But then, it was a Christmas movie.

"I hadn't heard much about him before this whole thing started with Joe Silvio," I said.

"He's been a landlord for years, and he was a slumlord before that," she said. "About five years ago the Metro County Council went after him for rental properties that had sofas and refrigerators in the yards, leaking ceilings and windows, overgrown grass with rats—all kinds of dilapidation. The codes department got all over him, and he finally set things right by tearing a lot of those places down and building new condos and affordable housing—with tax credits, which is what he was after all along."

"And he called my wine cheap," I said.

"Oh, he's a bad 'un. Now he uses that same formula to buy rundown places and build new ones through his construction companies. Word at the church—among some of the parishioners who move in those circles—is that he hires thugs to trash respectable places or harass the occupants so they will sell to him cheap."

"He really is Mr. Potter," I said. He seemed to feel bad about Joe Silvio, but I wondered if he would kill a man to get his wife to sell her place. The way his mind seemed to work, he would blame her for making it necessary.

I couldn't wait to get out of there, but I felt obligated to wait until everyone else had gone, until I made sure they were all right. I had given Stacie my cell and office numbers, but there were no messages from her. If Hatfield had contacted her, as he'd threatened, maybe she was going to deal with the fallout herself.

Which is as it should be.

Luke and Dani thanked me before leaving. They thanked me as a couple, her arm in his. He apologized again. I told them everything was fine. It was still raining mistily, as the day had begun, and there was a welcome quiet to the world.

Grant arrived at my house shortly after I did, bringing gifts of Thai takeout and French vanilla frozen yogurt. I kissed him, hugged him, and told him I did not honestly know what to eat first. We decided on actual food and set the containers on the old coffee table by the living room sofa.

"Still wound up about Brenda?" he asked.

It took me a second to figure out what he meant. "Brenda? No. That seems like yesterday."

"You've been busy?"

"Très."

I don't know why I drew on my high school French to answer. Probably because my brain was dead. Or maybe the hit on the head with a soup ladle had jogged it loose. I proceeded to tell him about my visit with Robert, my lunch with Stacie, and my teatime encounter with Stephen Hatfield. The last one troubled him.

"He's a bad man," Grant said.

"So everyone keeps telling me. But I'm guessing that is limited mostly to his business dealings."

"From what I hear, everything in his life is a business deal."

"To some degree. But while he doesn't think much of women as a gender, I believe he genuinely likes and certainly appreciates the ones he bonds with personally. He may be a serial monogamist, but he sounds like a loyal one."

Even so, I kept my cell phone near as we ate just in case Stacie called.

Grant told me that the case was still turning into dead ends.

"About the only thing certain I've got is the lab analysis of the wound on Joe Silvio's throat," he said. "It was made by a jeweler's screwdriver."

"Come again?"

"A jeweler's screwdriver with an eighth-inch-wide flat blade. Second and third stabs pierced the carotid artery. Seventh and eighth punctured the windpipe, though Joe was already unconscious by then."

"How many stabs were there?"

"Sixteen."

"Jesus."

"Somebody was pissed at Joe," Grant said. "We figure the dog came in around the tenth stab, since the blood had reached the shoulder blade, which is where the dog got to before it went between Joe's back and the seat."

"Do you know what kind of dog it was?"

He shook his head as he handed me the pad thai with chicken and took the curry chicken puffs. "That's the strange thing. Usually, you'll find strands of animal hair, but not this time. Nothing in the back of the truck, nothing on the back of the seat. No indentations in the bread or the vinyl of the seat from claw marks. Not even its territory marked on the tires. Zip. We can't account for it."

"Unless the killer was holding the dog," I said.

"We thought of that," Grant said. "But it would have been tough to do and inflict the wounds, especially if the guy was trying to defend himself. Which is also surprising. There are no defensive cuts on his hands."

Grant's description brought me back to that morning. Entering the truck from the back, stepping in the blood, finding the body sprawled in the seat. A deliveryman surprised by someone who got into the truck from the passenger's side or the back and . . .

Took out a jeweler's screwdriver and stabbed him to death while holding a dog?

"Do you think it was premeditated?" I asked.

"With a small screwdriver?"

"True."

"An argument? With a hitchhiker?"

"I don't know about a hitchhiker, but an argument with someone he may have known is our working theory," Grant said. "We've checked security cameras along the route he presumably took. Some places we see the truck, some not. He isn't stopped in any of the footage, and it's too dark inside to see if there's another passenger. So right now it's still just a theory."

"Who would Joe Silvio be arguing with?"

"No one who shows up on his home or office phone records," Grant said.

"What about his cell?"

"We're still waiting on those," he said.

"Does it usually take this long?"

Grant shook his head. "The chief gave it to McCoy at his request. He doesn't want to push until after the funeral."

"Is that a way to run an investigation?"

"No, but McCoy made a legitimate case. He said that it's possible there may be personally embarrassing information, which he would like to be able to present to Brenda before 'impersonal parties'—meaning me—get hold of it."

"Jeez, isn't that almost a confession that the guy was doing something he shouldn't've!"

"Not necessarily," Grant said. "It could be a legitimate abundance of caution on behalf of a bereaved member of an officer's family."

"Ah, more blue line stuff, huh?"

"Yes, but he gave us company records and logs that it

would've taken days and a subpoena to get. It's a knife that cuts both ways."

"Unlike a screwdriver, which only goes in and out," I said.

Grant winced.

"Autopsy turn up anything else?" I asked.

"Old appendix operation. Prostate cancer, pretty well along. He may not have known."

"Jeez."

"His doctor wasn't even aware of it. Said he'd had it years before, licked it," Grant said.

Poor guy. I was thinking about the screwdriver, the oddness of that—who the hell would carry such a thing?—when I blurted, "Holy crap!"

Grant dropped his chopsticks.

"Grant . . . Joe."

"What?"

"Joe's hands. Defensive wounds."

"I don't understand."

"Grant, he didn't have any cuts *or* dog bites, because he was wearing gloves. Deliverymen wear gloves. He didn't have any on when I found him. Someone took them."

He continued to look at me, even as he felt on the old carpet for his chopsticks. "You're right," he said.

"Damn straight. Think about it. A dog owner attacks someone. What does the dog do? Joins in, thinking the master is at risk. He attacks the victim."

"Who is so busy holding the dog away, the killer is free to perforate his throat!"

We resumed eating.

"That still doesn't tell us anything about the dog, though," Grant said. "The killer may not have been holding him. He could have been on his or her lap. That's why there are no claw marks."

"Well, at least we can rule out a stray," I said.

"We'd pretty much done that due to the lack of fur anywhere."

"Right."

We continued to eat and think in silence. Neither of us heard the car pull up until the doorbell rang. We jumped; I yelped. My cats, who had been lurking nearby, waiting to see if anything dropped to the floor, slunk away.

I looked out the peephole.

"It's Robert Reid," I told Grant.

"I assume you weren't expecting him?"

I shook my head as I opened the door. He was still dressed in white, holding a clear umbrella, roses, and a folder.

"Come in," I said.

He smiled his big smile, handed me the flowers, closed his umbrella and left it outside, then came in. He did a little double take when he saw Grant.

"See what you don't know when you don't have me followed?" I asked.

"I do indeed," he said.

Twenty-four hours ago this little vignette would have been my fantasy of the moment. Amazing what a difference a day can make.

"Care for some fried rice with pineapple?" I asked.

"No, but I'll take a ginger ale if you have one."

"I so happen not to," I said. "I may have a Diet 7UP."

"Even better," he said.

I went in the kitchen to get the drink and a glass and put the roses in water.

"How are you, Detective Daniels?" I heard him ask.

"Pretty well. Yourself?"

"I'm good. Keeping busy trying to find a killer."

"So Gwen has been telling me. Having any luck?"

"I'm not sure," he said as I returned. "That's why I'm here." He pulled up a slightly worn armchair to gather round the coffee table. "Just to be clear," he said to Grant, though he was looking at me, "I've apologized to Gwen for what I will charitably describe as a burst of exuberance in the methods I've used to try and cover this story."

"As far as I know, you didn't break any laws," Grant said diplomatically. "Just hassled a good friend."

"Guilty of one and"—he reached into the folder—"I'm afraid I may be guilty of the other."

Grant's chin came up.

"If I were smart and not so damn curious, I wouldn't do this in your presence," the bright-eyed publisher said to Grant. He handed me a sheet of paper. "This is a printout of calls made from Joe Silvio's cell phone."

Grant's mouth twisted. "When did you get those?"

"This morning," Robert said. "After Gwen left, I had a . . . well, a spare body to put on other kinds of research. I thought you would have obtained this list already and it was a waste of time and money, but you never know." He was studying Grant. Robert's features brightened. "Wait a minute. You *didn't* get them, did you?"

Grant's head went back and forth once.

"Interesting," Robert said.

I glanced at Grant. I gave him a look that said, "Knife cutting the wrong way." He nodded back, and then we looked at the list. A local number was circled in gold Sharpie.

"Recognize it?" Robert asked.

Grant shook his head. I told him I didn't know it, either.

"That makes three of us, but it's the night before the murder," Robert said. "Four hours before it happened, in fact. And the reason we don't know the number?"

"It's an off-the-rack phone," Grant said.

"Available at any number of local emporiums, that's correct," Robert said. "I'm wondering if our poor bread truck driver received a message, called back on the cell, and was, by this very phone call, lured to a meeting that led to his death. Lured by someone who either did not want to be traced or cannot afford a cell phone with a contract. But someone who knew him . . . and knew he would be making a delivery."

"That could be anyone at the bakery or in the deli," I said. "And that's just for starters."

"*Or* Joe may have had this cell phone number and initiated the call," Grant said. "He could have asked for what turned out to be the fatal rendezvous."

"It doesn't appear in any other records going back six months," Robert said.

"Which tells us nothing, *except* that Joe probably knew his killer and it was someone who had a beef with Joe personally," Grant said. "It was not a random killing."

Which still left the field wide open. Lydia's words came back to me just then, her response when I asked if she knew Joe Silvio: "A lot of folks down here knew him."

Chapter 21

The best laid plans of mice and men and love-starved women . . .

Robert didn't hang around much longer; he was trying very hard to be respectful and deferential to me. I didn't respect him any more for it, but I appreciated it. The poor little rich man climbed back into his vintage red Corvette a few minutes later, leaving Grant and me to finish our dinner and poke at the tub of frozen yogurt. Neither of us felt much like dessert of any kind.

I initiated the end-of-evening non-festivities.

"You can stay," I said, "but I think we should call it a night."

"I'm on board with that," he said.

It was what I wanted to hear. It was what I expected to hear. But Stephen Hatfield's words came back like a tsunami. In my world, there was no sex for sex's sake. I couldn't just say to Grant, "Hey, let's have a quick tumble. Then you can go to sleep. Or go. Whatever you want." If there was sex, he would stay, and if he stayed, there would be an implied "something" of a relationship or a familiarity, at least, in the morning, an obligation to be friendly or close or in some way committed.

There was a price for sex with me.

"The world is indeed off its axis if I'm quoting Hatfield to myself," I thought aloud as I went to bed. I was asleep within minutes—within minutes of 9:30 p.m., which was a measure of how tired I was—and was up with the sun.

In the light of day, the thing that seemed the strangest about the previous day was the thing about the jeweler's screwdriver. Who the hell carried one of those around? There weren't any jewelers on our long list of suspects.

I was about to leave for the deli when my cell rang. It was Grant.

"Bad news," he said. "That screwdriver belonged to Joe."

"What for?"

"According to McCoy, who asked his sister last night, he used it to make baseball displays for Dave's memorabilia shop. Kind of a hobby."

"So why was it in the truck?"

"He was going to tighten some of the stands during lunch. Apparently, they come loose when you screw and unscrew the plastic holders."

"Because . . . ?"

"People like to examine the signatures, make sure they're real and not printed. Anyway, Joe kept it in the ashtray so he wouldn't forget."

"Wow. Gotta say, I didn't see that coming," I said.

"If it's true, it tells me the killing wasn't planned."

"Yeah, but what a stupid, random way to die—because your ball screwing tool was in an ashtray to remind you to go somewhere."

"Would it have been better if it were a pen or pencil?"

"A little," I said. *Though Joe would still be just as dead.*

"But you were right about the gloves," he added.

"Brenda said he always wore them when he made deliveries. Good get, Gwen."

"Thanks."

I had no idea where the investigation was going after this, and I was glad it wasn't my responsibility.

I got to the deli early, figuring I owed it to the staff to beat everyone there and get as much of the prep work done as possible. Naturally, it didn't happen that way. I parked, and walking over, I saw a figure sitting on the front stoop, bent low, wearing a wrinkled hoodie. The rain had stopped, but the garment was damp; the person must have been there all night.

As I neared, I saw that it was Stacie.

"Jesus, girl," I said, hurrying the last few steps. I bent beside her, put my arms around her, helped her to her feet. Her head went back. Her cheeks were red, her skin was pale, and her eyes were bloodshot. Her hair was a scraggly mess under the hood. I didn't smell liquor on her breath, her pupils seemed normal, and her head wasn't rolling around.

"Sorry, sis," she said. "I didn't know where else to go."

"It's all right," I said, my arm around her waist as I shoved the keys in the door and pushed it open. I locked it behind us and helped her into a chair. "You're freezing," I said. "Let me make some coffee."

I ran behind the counter, tore open a packet of instant, and used hot water from the tap. I came back with the cup, a spoon, and a Danish on a plate. I placed them in front of her. I took off the sweatshirt and threw a man's sports jacket around her shoulders. Someone had forgotten it, and I kept it in my office. I never did figure out how a man forgot a sports jacket and didn't miss it.

"Eat," I said.

She picked up the pastry and took a bite.

"I'm sorry," she said again.

"Nothing to be sorry for. What happened?"

She snickered. "When? With who?"

"It doesn't matter. Talk."

She washed the pastry down with coffee.

"Good," she said. "Real good."

"I'm glad."

She took a long breath, seemed to recover slightly. "Okay. So I took your advice and wrote to Stephen that I wanted to see him. He wrote back, telling me I was ungrateful, and that it wasn't necessary to come and see him. Everything of mine that was at his house was really his, he said, so there was no reason to come back. He wished me well."

"What a prince," I said.

"I don't blame him," Stacie said. "It was pretty sudden. I don't regret it."

"Good for you."

"Maybe not." She smiled weakly. She ate more Danish. "When I got home, I made spaghetti for Scott—his favorite—and told him everything that had happened. About dating Stephen, about everything you said, about dumping Stephen. All of it. You know what he did? He started to cry."

"Did he say why?"

She shook her head, drank more coffee, added sugar, swirled it around. "He just cried for a while, and when I tried to comfort him, he told me not to. He stopped, picked at the spaghetti, had a little beer, cried some more—and then left."

"Had he ever cried before?"

"Only when he lost a hundred dollars on a Sting game."

"A what?"

"Charlotte Sting—women's basketball. It was the first and only time he bet. It was when he wanted to get me a nicer diamond for our engagement. Instead, he had to get me one that was a hundred dollars worse."

"I see."

"I went out looking for him. He had the car, so I ran for a while, going to the bars he usually visits. He had been to one of them, the Ghostly Booze, but he wasn't in any of them when I got there."

"Did you call the police?"

She nodded. She fought tears. "They found him beat up and unconscious on Harrison Street, by his car."

"My God. How is he?"

"He came to in the hospital but was real confused, not makin' any sense. They sedated him. I left, and . . . I came here."

"Do you think it was Hatfield?"

She drank her coffee and stared into her cup.

"Stacie?"

She looked over. "I don't know. He wouldn't take my call, and I knew he wouldn't let me in the gate. So I just sat, thinkin' that I had caused this to happen."

"No!" I leaned across the table and took her by the shoulders. "I talked to Scott, and I saw how heavy this thing weighed on him. I think he cried when you told him because he was relieved, and maybe a little ashamed, and he just didn't know how to handle it. After he left, he had a few drinks. Maybe he talked to the bartender. Maybe he got mad. Maybe he did something stupid. But *you* didn't cause that. You did the right thing by talking to him."

I hoped. I wasn't a shrink, and I'd made a couple of pop-psych suggestions based on a quick read of Scott and a quick read of Stacie. God help us all if I messed up.

One thing I needed to do, though, was get a picture of what happened after he left the bar.

"Will you be okay out here for a few minutes?"

She nodded.

"I'm sorry about all this," I said. "But we're going to make it all right."

"I believe you," she said.

I hurried to my office and shut the door. I had not, I'm ashamed to admit, torn up the business card Stephen Hatfield had left me. I had thought about it, more than I should have. It had a kind of electric power, like it was a conduit of the man. Even contemplating what he might have done, I found myself . . .

You're a sick girl, I chastised myself, though not hard enough.

I was actually aroused.

I took the man's card from my drawer, picked up the phone, and punched in his private number without hesitation. I was brave and jitter free when he was . . . I didn't even know how many miles away.

The phone rang. It was either late or too early by night-crawler standards. Either he was still up or I'd wake him. . . .

"Gwen Katz," he answered. "This is an unexpected surprise."

"Is it?"

"Completely."

"Just one question, Mr. Hatfield. Did you do anything to Scott Ferguson?"

There was a brief silence. "What is it you think I've done to him?" he asked.

"Had him beaten halfway to dead."

"Not me," he said.

He spoke with such certainty that I didn't know what to say next. Anger is good for marathon runs and multiple assaults; fury is only good for short sprints. I was furious and out of gas.

"Let me guess what happened," Hatfield said. "Our little cheerleader confessed all to her football hero, was met with relief and confusion and probably dollops of unhappiness, after which he toyed with the idea of confronting me in person. That is what jocks do, after all. First, though, he stopped at a local booze joint to fuel up. And then, tragically but perhaps fittingly, he ran afoul of some other jock or redneck or God knows who and had his ego, face, and vague plan rearranged. Would that not be an equally likely scenario?"

I didn't know what to say. Fortunately, I didn't feel obligated to say anything to this man. *Which was another thing,* I thought miserably. *I always feel like I have to talk to Grant about something. Anything.*

"Gwen? Are you there?"

"Sorry to have wakened you," I said, chilled by the double entendre I found in *that*.

"No problem. I go to bed rather early when there's no one to keep me awake."

"Creepy."

"Excuse me?"

"Nothing," I said. "I have to go."

I could see him smile. He could probably see me squirm.

"You *do* fascinate me," he said. "I hope you will consider dinner some night. Out, if you feel safer."

"Thanks. I don't think so."

"That's the problem," he said.

"What is?"

"Don't think."

I hung up. The conversation had gone on about four exchanges too long. My hand was still on the receiver. It was shaking. I wished to hell I could follow my own advice and talk about what was inside me right now. But I didn't know. He was wrong. I had done things without thinking. My first, the professor, was one—a big one. A no-returns-accepted impulse buy my freshman year. That was probably why I was so cautious now: that one did major damage.

You have never talked to anyone about that. Not even Phil, who didn't want to hear about the men who came before. It is long overdue. Maybe now that you have a sister who has been in similar shoes . . .

My eyes fell on a scrap of paper in the corner of my desk. The writing blasted Stephen Hatfield out of my brain and into next week.

"Not possible," I said, thinking back. "Not . . . no. How does that even fit?"

I went to call Grant, realized he wasn't the man I needed to talk to. I turned on my monitor, looked up another number. It was early, but that was too damn bad.

I took a quick trip to the dining area. "Stacie, are you all right?"

"Can I get myself another coffee?"

"Of course. Behind the counter in a box marked Maxwell House."

She nodded.

She was all right enough. I went back to the office and picked up the phone.

As for Robert Reid, he would take my call and like it.

Chapter 22

"The list?" he said groggily.

"The phone list," I repeated. "From last night. The one with the calls from Joe Silvio's cell phone."

"Oh, right," he said. "What time is it?"

"Nearly six," I said.

He yawned loudly. "That's why I run a family newspaper. Woodward and Bernstein hours blow."

I didn't touch the line. I was too distracted. I was pretty sure I was right. I just couldn't make the pieces fit.

"Robert, get the hell up and do your damn job. The job your daddy's trust fund pays you for."

"No need to get personal," he said.

"Oh, there's every need. Finding a killer and doling out payback to you, which is going to be a gift that keeps on giving."

"I'm going," he said. "The list is in my jacket, I think. Which is in the car."

I heard shuffling sounds. A robe, slippers. Maybe he was shushing a lover.

God, what if he's no different than Stephen Hatfield, festooning his bed with boy toys like that receptionist in his lobby, giving them gifts, then discarding them when

*he's through? Why does that behavior seem somehow
more acceptable in his world than in mine? Why do the
young men who take his trinkets seem smart, canny,
not used?*

Then I thought, *Why can you think so clearly about
his imaginary love life and not your own? Because—
drumroll, cue Stephen Hatfield—it's just about the sex,
as far as you know.*

Then I thought, *You're being an idiot. How do you
know any of what you just thought is true? For all you
know, he may be in a long-term committed relationship.*

"I'm going," he said. "It's in the garage."

"You leave your clothes in the garage?"

"When I get home late," he said.

"Go out partying?"

"Huh? No. I was reviewing the files my PIs compiled
for me. Hey, did you know Scott Ferguson got into a
fight last night?"

"Where? Do you know why?"

"Some guy was being too attentive to a cocktail waitress at the Ghostly Booze Bar. Scott offered her a ride
home. The guy was a biker with the Muscles for Anarchy motorcycle club. Bodybuilding bikers. Three of
them surrounded him outside the park. One took the
girl. The others trashed him. Wrong iron crosses to
cross."

*Not if you have something to prove or feel like you
should be punished for something, or both,* I thought.

"Catchy headline, don't you think?" he said self-
admiringly.

"Where are you?" I asked.

"I'm going as fast as I can on two hours' sleep. What
is this, anyway?"

"I'll let you know if I'm right."

He went the rest of the way in silence. I heard room

doors open and close. I heard a car alarm beep. I heard that door open. I heard more rustling.

"Okay," he said. "You ready?"

I looked at the desk. "Ready."

He read the number. I swore. It matched.

"So?" he asked.

I said, "Guess what? I'm right."

"Sweet! Whose number is it?"

I replied, "I said I'd let you know if I was right. I was. Bye."

"Dammit, Gwen—"

I hung up. And felt very good about it, I did.

I was wired. "Priorities," I said.

I decided to give Grant five more minutes of sleep. I went into the dining room. Stacie was back in her chair, huddled over her second cup of instant.

"Let me make some of the real stuff," I said.

"This is okay—"

"For me," I said.

I worked with filters and a bag of McNulty's behind the counter. They were from a coffee bean store on Christopher Street in the West Village. I'd been buying beans there since my student days. I wasn't about to stop drinking Bavarian Chocolate Cherry just because I'd moved to another world.

"I have some news," I said.

She looked up hopefully. I guess my tone of voice told her it wasn't bad news, for once.

"Scott was hurt because he tried to defend a server at that bar last night," I said.

"He did?"

"Yes indeed. From the Muscles for Anarchy motor-cycle club."

"Bikers? He's hated them since high school!"

"Well, he got it out of his system last night," I told

her. "Maybe he was doing for himself what you did for yourself. Had to express something he'd been keeping inside."

"God, the MFA," she said.

The big machine was locked and loaded, and I switched it on. The blurping sound filled the room, followed by the incomparable smell of fresh-brewed. I went back to her table.

"Why don't you go see him?" I said. "Stay with him?"

"I—I can't. Work."

"Does Sammi have anyone else she can call?"

"Sure, but I need the paycheck."

"Not from there," I said.

"Sorry?"

"Why don't you come to work here?" I asked, not quite sure I was doing the right thing. But I was taking my own advice: it was what was inside. I was just laying it out.

"Are you serious?"

"Pretty much all the time," I said ruefully.

She jumped up and hugged me and ran her left hand up and down my spine and wept and probably would have stayed there if I hadn't put my hands on her arms and gently pushed her back.

"Why don't you call her and explain what happened?" I suggested. "I'm sure she'll understand. Then you can stop by later and give your two weeks' notice."

She lunged at me again. "Thank you, sister. Thank you."

"You're welcome," I said.

She finished the Danish and drank more coffee, and then—showing promise—took the cup and dish back to the sink, which she found without having to ask.

"I'll call you," she said as she took off the jacket and grabbed her damp sweatshirt. "I love you."

"Talk to you later, Stace," I said.

I wasn't quite at that same gushing level. Stacie to Stace was about the best I could do then.

I let her out, locked the door behind her, then went to the office. I called Grant on his cell. He answered groggily.

"Hey," he said.

"Hey," I replied.

Shit, damnation, and Faust. That was lame buddy talk.

"How are you this morning?" he asked.

"Good."

And more of the same.

"Guess what?" he said, without waiting for me to buddy-answer, "What?" "I called the chief at home last night. Told him about the Silvio cell phone list. McCoy's in for an internal affairs investigation after the funeral."

"Now I've got news for you," I said. "That cell phone number on Reid's list? It belongs to Lydia Knight."

I could hear the intake of air. I recognized intake from outflow from sex. Our lovemaking was at the same level as our more interesting conversation.

"Does Robert know?"

"He knows that *I* know, but he doesn't know *what* I know."

"Thank you," Grant said. "Crap. I'm going to need that list in order to get a search warrant. We should have it this morning. How do you know it's Lydia's number?"

"She wrote it down for me."

"You have it in her handwriting?"

"I do."

"That may be enough to get the process rolling," he said. "Can I come by?"

"I'm at the deli," I said.

"See you in a few."

Chapter 23

I flipped on the deep fryers to let them heat up, sliced fresh onions, brought in the bread when it was delivered from McCoy's. I had decided it would be wrong to change suppliers permanently, even though there was a wary chill from Pete, my regular delivery guy. Polite "How do?" and a formal "Sign please," even though I knew the drill.

Grant knocked on the door a half hour after our talk. He was wearing the same clothes as the night before and looked a little wan.

"Been at it all night?" I asked as we went to the office.

"More or less," he said. "Caught a couple hours of power nap at my desk."

"It's scary when the habits of you and Robert Reid align."

He didn't seem to hear. I had handed him the paper on which Lydia had written her number.

"This doesn't mean she did anything but get a call from him," he pointed out.

I knew that monotone of his. He was actually talking to himself, working through this.

"His last call before letting you know he was going to be late," he said.

I heard the door key turn the latch. I looked out, waved at Thomasina. She had seen Grant's car out front and went about finishing what I'd started in the kitchen. She hummed as she worked.

It must be nice to be happy, I thought. *Or at least content.*

"I'm wondering what connection they could possibly have," I said. "It seems kind of random. I mean, she said she knew him from church, but that's no reason for an early morning phone call."

"There's nothing else in the records," he said. "Not even a photo of them together."

I said, because that was the way everything seemed to be going, "Affair?"

"Of course it's possible," he agreed, "though I'd be real surprised. We talked to folks at Silvio's church. He was deep into the congregation, Bible studies, fund-raising. I don't think it was for show. He seemed devout."

"Even devout men have needs, and Brenda is kind of . . . I dunno. A tad formal? You're a man. What do you think?"

"I think I'd rather be with you," he said.

That was supposed to be a compliment. He was too tired to see how it fizzled.

He took the number, kissed my cheek—another strike—and hurried off to see about getting a judge on the phone. I went over to Thomasina.

"Who was the guest?" she asked, looking up from the ketchup dispensers she was filling and nodding at the sink.

I filled her in. After all, she was like a surrogate mother to Stacie.

"Lawsy, the poor child," she said.

"Poor, but soon to be among friends and family," I said.

Thomasina looked at me as though she had X-ray vision and could see into my head. "You hired her?"

"I did."

I have to admit, I wasn't sure how she'd react. Would she think I was dragging old wounds front and center, putting an explosive vest to our bosom, or was I dutifully, lovingly helping family?

The big woman nodded approvingly. "Good for you, Nash dear. God *bless* you, and good for you."

That was a relief. I still couldn't be sure I'd made the right decision, but I was surer than I was ten seconds ago.

The rest of the staff trickled in, Luke and Dani arriving together. I felt like I was watching a science fiction TV show about a time slip. Every time I saw them, their dynamics had jumped to a new level. They walked to the counter, arms around each other's waist, oblivious to everyone else until we said good morning. Then they broke and went about their business but never seemed to lose eye contact.

As we neared the opening bell, there was a rap on the door. Thomasina was opening the cash register, and I was in the office. I heard the keys turn. I heard my manager talking. I couldn't hear who she was talking to. Probably an early customer. If we were ready, we usually let them in.

A minute later her big frame filled the door.

"Nash?"

"Yes?" I looked over from our Web site. I'd been thinking about revamping it, and actively working on that now stopped me from thinking about "my buddy" Grant.

"You have a visitor," Thom said. "Lydia."

Speak of the angel of maybe death, I thought. "Coming," I said.

Thom left, and I gathered myself.

What could she want? I wondered. To thank me for helping Stacie? Had her daughter called to tell her what I'd done? Had Lydia heard about Scott, about Stephen Hatfield? Or maybe she was headed to Joe Silvio's funeral. The good news was, wearing her usual wardrobe, she was already dressed for it.

She was standing by the cash register like a customer waiting to be seated. There was a leash attached to a parking meter outside and a wirehair fox terrier attached to the leash. It was sitting, panting, staring after its master.

Lydia seemed calm. I hoped she wouldn't try to kiss me. I made a point of stopping just outside of hugging range.

"Good morning," I said.

"Hello, dear," she said.

"What can I do for you?"

She smiled. It was the smile of a woman who seemed at peace. "I was walking the dog before work and decided to stop by."

So much for mourning Joe Silvio, I thought.

"Stacie came to the shoe store after work," she said. "She told me you'd taken her to lunch and had a lovely talk. That warmed me, Gwen. The fact that she spoke to me after being so cross was . . . What was the word your father used? A mitzvah."

That made my flesh crawl.

"Stacie also told me I didn't have anything to worry about in that other matter."

"No," I said. "That's through."

"I'm so glad," she said.

There was something missing here, though. She

seemed a little too calm, given what had happened since. It might not have been my place, but . . .

"Lydia, did you hear about Scott?"

Her expression clouded. "Scott? What about him?"

I said, "He had a run-in with some gang members. He's in the hospital."

She put her hand to her mouth. "Poor boy! Is he badly hurt?"

"I think he'll recover," I said. "I'm surprised Stacie didn't tell you."

"Oh, well, I'm sure she was busy and . . . well, she couldn't have," Lydia said.

"Why not?"

"You see, that's actually the reason I stopped by," she said. "That cell phone number I gave you? You wouldn't have been able to reach me."

"Why?"

"Lord, I hate those things. I guess I'm just old-fashioned."

"Fine, but why would I not have been able to reach you?"

"I got it at a RadioShack to keep in my bag for emergencies, and touch wood, I haven't had one," she said. "So I didn't even realize it's been missing, for only God knows how long."

Chapter 24

Lydia's little flyby threw me into a tailspin. Here, I had thought we had not just a killer but a killer who I didn't like. Sure, it would have hurt Stacie to know her mother was homicidal—but it also would have been a fitting capper to a lifetime of disappointment.

So the cell phone was lost. Or stolen. I went to the office and called the number. There was no answer.

Crud.

I thought of the only light-fingered cell phone thief I knew—Scott Ferguson. He had access, but what was the motive? What could he possibly have against Joe Silvio? Being fired for having sex in a bread truck?

I phoned Grant to tell him the latest. He seemed a little crestfallen to hear it.

"I thought we might have this cat in a bag," he said.

"Sorry," I told him.

"Not your fault," he said consolingly. It was flat, hollow. God, was everything he said going forward going to seem bland? What had that sicko Hatfield done to me?

He was going to go ahead with the search warrant, since there was still enough cause to have it in hand.

We opened. Working the cash register, I noticed people passing slowly by the big window that had our name written large in red. They were well dressed, looking in with sour expressions and then moving on. It was like a scene from a Bergman film—the one I'd actually stayed awake through, anyway.

Then I realized who they were: Silvio mourners. The funeral home was a few blocks north, and they were passing by to see where it had happened . . . and, perhaps, to brand me with their pissy expressions. I wanted to stick my tongue out at everyone who looked my way.

And then it occurred to me.

There is one person who might have some insight, I thought. I looked at my watch. I had about forty-five minutes. I should probably wear a Kevlar vest for what I had in mind, but I was going to do this.

I asked Thom to man the cash register—she did not seem surprised—and went out the door without bothering to get my bag. I didn't expect to be gone very long, unless I got myself arrested.

The Dumas Funeral Home was located on Third Avenue South. I literally ran all the way over, feeling like my dad's hero, the New York Giants' scrambling quarterback Fran Tarkenton.

The glum faces didn't recognize me as I overtook them on their way from the parking garage. They merely looked at me like I was crazy, which I probably was. I trotted past the outside usher, stopped to sign the register so I could catch my breath, then looked into the chapel for Brenda Silvio. She was in the front pew with her brother.

This was going to be ugly. Not only wouldn't I be welcome, but I also wasn't dressed for the occasion.

"I need to talk to you," I said, cutting into a little hemisphere of family and friends.

Jason looked like the embodiment of that demon I said I let loose. He was the kraken made landfall.

"Get out!" he said, grabbing the wrist that was nearest him.

I yanked it hard from his thick grip. "Brenda, I need to talk to you."

The woman looked up through her veil. Her mouth was so tight, it looked like it might shatter. For all I knew, her teeth already had and she was just keeping them inside.

"Ushers!" Jason called back.

"We need to talk about Lydia Knight. *Now,*" I said.

Two beefy ushers arrived. Brenda held them, and her brother, off with a hand. I envied the power in those five little fingers.

"Is there somewhere this person and I can talk?" she asked an usher. "Alone?"

"Yes," he said and extended a practiced arm.

Brenda rose slowly, unsteadily, helped by her brother. He walked with her to a small room off the chapel—it probably had an official name, but I had no idea what that was. I had gone past the closed white coffin, semi-oblivious, though the widow slowed to brush her hand across the side as she passed. It was a sweet gesture. I hoped it was sincere. I wanted to believe it. I had no reason not to believe it.

Was I that desperate for romance that I got warm and fuzzy watching a woman I didn't like and her dead husband?

Apparently.

Jason fired a warning-shot look across my bow as he settled his sister into a pale green armchair and backed out of the room. The usher had remained at the door. He shut it with a quiet click. Everything was quiet in here, even the floorboards.

Well . . . funeral home. Death.

Brenda glared up at me. "What do you want?"

"One of the last calls your husband made from his cell phone on the night of his death was to Lydia Knight," I said.

She looked up at me with a look that was half disbelief, half horror. "I don't believe you."

"Ask your brother," I said. "Go ahead. Call him in. He suppressed Joe's cell phone records."

I could hear Grant swearing at me in my imaginary future; I didn't care, I didn't know why I didn't care, and I didn't care about that, either.

"Why would he do that?" Brenda asked.

"I don't know," I admitted. "To avoid a scandal? Or the hint of a scandal? To protect you?"

"From what?" she said. "Joe wasn't a philanderer. He was a devoted husband and a devout, churchgoing man."

"So I've heard," I said. "Still, he called Lydia's cell phone a few hours before he was murdered."

She was clearly struggling to process the implications of what I'd told her. A unified theory eluded her. "Go on," she said.

"I know this is difficult, but did they have any kind of relationship or friendship or anything? Ever?"

"I don't see how that's any business of yours," Brenda said hotly.

"Lydia had a longtime affair with my father," I said.

"That is not news," she fired back.

"I guess not. Apparently, I'm the only one in Nashville who was unaware of the great Katz legacy. Lydia is also the mother of my half sister—though you probably know that, too."

Brenda did not acknowledge that one.

"That's the 'business of mine' that Lydia Knight is.

That, and the fact that the call sort of makes her a suspect in Joe's murder."

"Why drop this in my lap an hour before my husband's funeral? Why don't you ask her?"

"Because I'm not sure I trust her," I said. "I trust you. We may not like each other, but I've done business with your company—with you—for nearly a year. I believe you're an honest woman."

That seemed to soften her a little. Not much, but enough to get her to talk to me.

"Talk to me," I said. "I can call Detective Daniels to come down and ask these questions, *or* we can talk about this woman to woman, I can pass along anything relevant, and you can get on with your mourning."

"You take a lot upon yourself," she said.

"Story of my life," I replied. "Brenda, what was Lydia Knight to your husband?"

She sighed long and deep. There were tears.

For Joe? I got the feeling they weren't. It was his funeral, but she hadn't been crying before.

"Before Joe and I married, he had a brief relationship with Lydia," Brenda said. "She had been dating your father, was upset that he wouldn't marry her, and . . . well, she started seeing other men."

You two-timing bitch, I thought, ignoring the fact that I was nearly about to do that to Grant, except the other guy turned out to like guys.

"So Joe was one of her revenge dates," I said.

"I suppose he was. Then he proposed to me. The relationship ended."

"I'm sorry, but I have to ask—"

"Am I sure it ended?" she said. She laughed a little. "I'm sure. Joe . . . Joe was a man of some innocence."

What the hell did *that* mean?

"I'm not following," I said.

"Lydia was his first. I was his second. And his last. I know that."

"Because he went to church? That's your evidence?"

"No," she said.

"What, then?"

I was watching her as she wept. There were a *lot* of tears. That was to be expected at her husband's funeral, but I wondered if there was something else. These were coming from her belly, not her chest. She was heaving. *Guilt.*

And then it occurred to me.

"Twice a day," I said.

"Pardon?"

"The calls to Dave. You two dated in high school. You were the one phoning him."

She cried harder.

"You were seeing him."

She nodded.

"Did Joe know?"

"I don't think so."

"Brenda, did Dave—"

"No!" she exclaimed through the tears. "Dave and I both loved Joe! They loved one another, and they both loved me! Dave would *never* have done anything to hurt either of us."

Except screw his best friend's wife, I thought.

"All right, fine," I said. "Then back to Lydia. How do you know Joe hadn't seen her again, that he was faithful?"

"Because," she said, "he had cancer a year after we were married."

I didn't tell her I knew that. I let her continue at her own pace.

"The doctors operated," she said. "They cured him. But when they were down there, they nicked a nerve."

"Oh," I said. The coroner had obviously missed that. "So he couldn't—"

"Not after that," she said.

So good friend Dave stepped in for his impotent friend. Men were so giving.

"We just found out, only a few days before—before *this* happened—that the cancer had returned," Brenda said. "Joe tried to hide it, but I knew how upset he was. That was why I was so short with you on the phone. It wasn't a good week."

"I'm sorry," I said. So they did know about the recurrence. "Brenda, do you think that's why Joe may have been talking to Lydia? To let her know?"

"I don't know," she said. "Why would he? They hadn't spoken for years. I don't even shop in her store."

The door pushed open. Jason looked in.

"Brenda? Are you all right?"

"Yes," she said, taking control of herself.

"We need you out here," he said, firing eye daggers at me.

"I'm coming," she said. The woman reached for a box of tissues, pulled out several, and touched the wad to her eyes. She had been expecting to cry. She hadn't worn mascara. "Excuse me," she said and rose.

"Of course," I said. "Thank you."

She didn't respond. She just looked away, not with anger but with sadness. I accepted that. For us, that was something of a breakthrough.

Chapter 25

There was a back door from the secret room, and I took it.

My head was awhirl with Brenda, Joe, and Dave. It was like the song in *The Mikado*. "Here's a how-de-do! . . . Here's a pretty mess."

The key to this how-de-do was Lydia's cell phone. Who had it?

I thought of calling Grant or even Robert to see if they could do some kind of triangulation thing, but it occurred to me that if someone had used it to lure Joe to his death, they would have discarded it by now.

Which would also include Lydia, of course.

My brain went to people who had been off to the side of the radar. Jason, for instance. Covering up evidence, maybe looking to clear the way for his sister to be with a guy who could perform. He could've gone to chat with Joe before his own shift, got into an argument with the man, and . . .

Stabbed him with a jeweler's screwdriver?

That didn't seem like Jason McCoy's style. And then there was the dog. He wouldn't have been going to work with Hitch or Macguffin. Or come to the heart of Nashville to walk them.

I was distracted the rest of the workday. There were moments of relief, like when Stacie called to say that despite a concussion, a broken nose, a trio of cracked ribs, and a black-and-blue face, Scott was going to be okay. Another small victory for true love. She asked if we could have dinner. I told her sure, I'd love to, and I'd meet her at the hospital around seven.

I did things by rote. My body was in the game, but my head was on Brenda and Joe, on Dave and Brenda, on Joe and Dave, on Lydia and Joe, on Brenda and Jason. There was a combination there that I believed was not a healthy one.

It was conceivable, I thought, that having gone through cancer once, Brenda might want to spare her husband the agony of a new round of treatments. She knew his route. Maybe she and one of the dogs went with him.

And then she euthanized him . . . with the screwdriver and dog? And took his gloves as a keepsake?

Would Dave have done that? Then there was still the little old phone thief Scott, though he would have had to borrow a dog. All roads led to one place, but I couldn't make it stick. Especially if . . .

"But what if she did?"

It didn't tell me *why,* but it was the only reasonable *who.*

I wasn't going to go over now. I would wait until closing. This was not something you did with people around. Like dressing down a worker, you took them to the woodshed. Otherwise, both of you were just putting on a show.

I worked on cleanup, sent the staff home when we

were nearly done, then went to my office to check the address.

Lydia saved me the trouble. There was a knock at the door, and I let her in.

"*Qu'elle* coincidence," I said, still puzzled by my pseudo-French. I must be longing for the more innocent days of eighth grade. "I was just about to come and see you."

"I thought you might." She invited herself into the office. *My* office.

I followed her in. She stood by my chair and faced me. I stood in the doorway in case I had to bolt.

"Why did you think I would come to see you?" I asked.

"Because you have questions," Lydia said. "You *do* have questions, don't you? You must. I saw you talking to Brenda this morning."

"You did?"

"Of course. I attended the service. It would have been graceless not to. Why would you, of all people, be talking to her then, there, if you didn't have important *questions?*"

She said the word with a hint of anger. I looked across my desk. There were pencils, pens, and untwisted paper clips on the desk. Any one of them could be a lethal weapon in skilled or maniacal hands.

"So why were you coming to see me?" Lydia asked.

"To tell you that I didn't think anyone took your phone."

"Why do you think that?"

"Because you remembered the number when you wrote it down. I can't remember my own number, and I actually give it out to people. That phone wasn't in your bag just for emergencies."

She hesitated for the briefest instant, then said, "That is true."

"Why did you lie?" I asked her.

"Because I didn't know how to explain my conversation with Joe. But then I was thinking, 'Here is a woman who told my daughter to speak the truth. She would appreciate the truth.'"

"Which is?"

"Joe was very ill, with cancer," she said.

"How did you know?"

"He told me," Lydia said. "That night."

"Why you? You weren't having an affair?"

"Oh no," she said. "Joe was a rock. A soft one, pyrite, but a rock nonetheless."

That was cold. "Isn't pyrite a metal?"

"No, dear. A mineral. You're thinking of gold."

I smirked. "You seem to know something about jewelry."

I thought I saw her eyes narrow just a bit. It was difficult to say since they were already pretty slitty.

"So why did you talk to Joe that night?"

"Because he wanted to make a clean breast of things."

"With you? Why, if that was years ago—"

"Not with me," she said through her teeth. "With my daughter. With *our* daughter."

Whatever you may hear during the course of your life that makes you feel as though you want to throw up a week's worth of meals, it couldn't hit half as hard as that statement hit me. It wasn't just that she had lied to me, to Stacie; it was the implications to both of us going forward. Still, some part of my brain was still on the job.

"The adoption," I said. "That was Joe?"

"That was Joe."

"Did Brenda know he was trying to adopt his own baby?"

"I believe she did," Lydia said. "That's why she forbade it. How was she to know she would never be able to have a child of her own? At least, not by her husband."

"The other night," I said. "The night of the call."

"He told me he wanted to tell her. I implored him to let me speak with him face-to-face. He told me he would pick me up in the truck. He had to get here by a certain time. He was devoted to his customers. I went to meet him. I brought the dog he had given Stacie for one of her birthdays. We argued. I tried to explain how I had been working up the courage to come and see you. It wasn't easy, you know. You were the daughter of the only man I ever loved, the man by whom I truly wanted a child."

"You lied and told my father the baby was his."

"I did," she said, as unrepentant as an Occupy Wall Streeter. "I had wanted to meet you ever since you came down here. I was so nervous. You saw that first day I couldn't even cross the street."

"That had nothing to do with what went on behind the deli?"

The narrow eyes opened a little. Tears formed on the sides, rolled along her cheek. I was unmoved. I was ready to spit fire.

"Joe didn't want to continue with the lie," I said.

"Give me a moment," Lydia said. "This isn't easy."

"I'm sure it isn't. You're about to confess to murder. You sat in the passenger's seat, the dog on your lap, and when he told you his decision was final, you grabbed the nearest sharp object you could find and plunged it in his neck. The dog joined in then, his hands went up to protect himself from *that,* and between the barking and the rage and the years of hurt and concern for Stacie, you just kept punching holes in his throat. You probably don't even remember doing it."

"I don't!" she wailed. "I truly don't!"

"Until you saw the dog lapping his blood. Then you came around. You took his gloves, the murder weapon, maybe even made sure there was no dog hair on the seat, then left. You went so fast, the dog didn't even have time to pee on the damn truck!"

She cried into her left hand. She reached for me with her right. I took a step back. I didn't want her to touch me.

Lydia looked up from her palm. "I'm so, so sorry! I did it for Stacie! So she could have the family she never had, a better life. Scott will never be able to support her, just as your father was never able to support me. I wanted something better for her. I knew you could show her, help her."

"Especially if I thought she was my goddamned sister."

"Yes. I believed that."

"So you lied and killed, and now . . . *now* you're going to take her on a trip through Robert Reid's tabloid journalism when you stand trial for murder."

"That's why I came to you," she said. "I want to go away. She never needs to know the truth. Let her think she's your blood. Joe felt he was going to die. I didn't do anything terribly wrong."

"You are seriously cracked."

"I did this for Stacie, *not* for myself!" she screamed. "I want nothing, other than to go away. The crime doesn't need to be solved! She need never know any of this!"

I heard a sound to my right and looked over. The nausea I had felt before returned. Stacie was standing a few feet away, her face like something from the sketch-book of Edvard Munch. She approached slowly.

"Scott was asleep, so I left the hospital early," she said.

"Stacie?" Lydia cried.

"How is he?" I asked softly.

"Talking when he isn't sipping juice through a straw," she said. Her mouth was working, but her expression was one of shock.

"Why don't you sit down in the dining room?" I said. "I'll come over—"

She shook her head firmly and stood beside me. She looked into the office. "Mother, what have you done?"

"No! Go away!"

"You killed . . . my *father?*"

However fallen Stacie's face looked, it was nothing like the vision of utter, contorted horror that overcame the face of her mother. She screamed a sound I hoped I never heard again as she fell in the seat, her head flopping back, still wailing. I put an arm across the doorway to keep Stacie back, and I stepped in—just as Lydia bent forward, reached for a pair of scissors I had in a pencil holder, and tried to push it into her chest.

Yes, I got between her and the blades and took them in the right arm.

Stacie jumped in after me, pulled her mother's hand away, and pinned it to the wall behind her. I reached up, grabbed the scissors, threw them to the floor, and put my hands around Lydia's other arm, which was clawing at her daughter's back. My right arm ached like I had a muscle cramp, but we managed to immobilize her. Stacie put her knee against her mother's waist, pushed the chair against the wall, and took the arm I was holding.

"I've got her," Stacie said. "Call nine-one-one."

I backed away. I couldn't get to the desk phone, and I didn't feel like dragging myself to the cash register, so I fished out the phone nearest me.

The one I saw in Lydia's purse.

Chapter 26

I needed a trip to the emergency ward.

The blades had cut the skin but had only glanced off the muscle, so five stitches would fix me right up. Grant arrived moments after the first responders. But before they took me away, he supervised the custody taking of Lydia Knight, made sure Stacie was all right—she was sitting at the counter, sobbing into her folded arms, but he let her be—then came over while the EMTs were bandaging me.

"We can get her statement later," he said.

"Thanks."

"Yours too. When did you plan to bring me in on this?"

"Soon," I said.

"Your independence is a challenge," he said.

Wrong thing to say, Detective Daniels. Seriously wrong.

"I didn't even know you went to the memorial today," he said. "And I was there."

"You must've come late. Lydia saw me."

"I arrived after you slipped through an exit in the side chapel."

That's what the little room is called? How disappointing.

"You seem to have made a friend, though," Grant went on. "Jason McCoy was furious at what you did, but Brenda shut him up. She said you were kind and very respectful."

I was, I thought.

Grant looked around. He went to the office and gave it a once-over. There was really nothing left for us to say—about this and probably about anything else. I don't even know if he sensed that. He came back, gave me a kind of formal good-bye, then left to see to Lydia Knight's booking.

I guess maybe he did know.

When the paramedics were finished, I took a moment to go where Stacie was sitting. I took the stool beside her, easing my wounded arm onto the counter.

"Hi," I said.

She looked up and struggled to find a little smile. "You know something? That was the first thing you said to me."

"That's why I said it. Because we're going to start over from right here. You may not be my sister by blood—or half blood—but we can still be good friends. Close friends. Who our fathers are doesn't matter."

"You don't think so?"

"I know so. What we've just been through? What still lies ahead of us? We are bonded for life."

Stacie slipped toward me, snaked her tear-dampened arms around my shoulders, and wept. I put my arms around her and did the same.

She might have gone about it as wrong as a human being could possibly do anything, but Lydia Knight had achieved her goal.

Chapter 27

I woke up famished.

After getting stitches in the emergency room, I had gone home without eating, had passed out, and woke only when Thomasina called to tell me to get my butt to the deli. I asked her to please, please have two toasted bagels with lox and cream cheese waiting for me.

I got there to find my order on the table nearest the door, right beside a newspaper that lay open.

Most people reading the paper this morning would be poring over the headlines about the arrest of Lydia Knight. Here only one story mattered. It was on page two, and it was the *Nashville National*'s 2012 Best & Worst list.

Halfway down, in Arial black type, it said:

Best Mid-Range Restaurant: Murray's Deli

"Oh my God!" I blurted.

Robert Reid walked over, applauding. He reached into his messenger bag and pulled out a plaque boasting VOTED BEST OF 2012 BY THE *NASHVILLE NATIONAL*.

"Oh my God!" I repeated.

That was when I heard the staff and our breakfast customers applauding as they watched and smiled. I returned the salute, applauding—with one hand against my thigh, since the other arm was a little incapacitated—as I locked eyes with each and every employee.

"Thank you so much," I said to Robert. "Uncle Murray would be so proud."

"He would indeed," he said. "Of the restaurant, of the award, and of you."

I frowned. "Brownnosing won't get you an interview."

"Will it get me a dinner?"

"Without an interview?"

"How about . . . Can we at least talk about one?"

"Maybe," I said. "With three conditions."

"Name them."

"First, you have to swear to me that this award had nothing to do with giving you an interview."

"It did not," he assured me. "We voted before I heard the news of the murder being solved. By you. One of our city's best and brightest and bravest—"

"Knock it off."

"Done," he said. "What's the second condition?"

"We take my . . . my dear new employee Stacie. For whom you will buy a dress and some bling for the event."

"I'll make that happen," he said. "You *are* talking about—"

"The Stacie who is working for me," I said. "You do not, will not, won't even think about talking to her. That is my third condition."

"Met," he said. "When do you want to do this?"

"I'll check with her and let you know," I said. I smiled, held up the plaque. "Thanks for this."

He smiled back. "You earned it, honey."

I went to my office, accompanied by cheers and Thomasina's big smile. I paused to give my manager a hug.

New York was wonderful for so many reasons. I was formed there. I experienced so much there, both good and bad. I gathered the information that, going forward, would help to make me a happier, more fulfilled human being, a good employer, and a better friend to the people near and dear to me.

However, there *is* one thing they don't have there and never will.

Murray's.

Best Mid-Range Restaurant of the Year.

Note: When Murray the Pastrami Swami passed away, hundreds of delectable recipes passed away with him. However, his uncle Moonish from Romania opened his own delicatessen on Manhattan's Lower East Side in 1919—where he hung a sign that said MY HERRINGS ARE SO FRESH, YOU'LL HAVE TO SLAP THEM. Uncle Moonish taught Murray everything he knew. Uncle Moonish also wrote down his recipes for posterity. He had so much trouble learning the new language of his adopted country that one waiter in Moonish's delicatessen put up a sign that said ENGLISH BROKEN HERE.

These recipes were passed down to his son Murray, who promptly misplaced them. Then, a few years ago, I found them among Murray's possessions—including a stringless ukulele and a signed photo of Alice Faye—that were stored in my aunt Shelia's attic on Long Island.

So now you, lucky readers, can re-create one of these delectable recipes as a treat for the whole family. I've updated the recipe where necessary, but here it is, in Uncle Moonish's own words.

SAUERKRAUT
(Make your own. Why pay someone to make it?)

Ingredients:

- 2 nice heads of cabbage. Each cabbage should be the size of Melnick the Fish Peddler's head. They need to be cored and nicely shredded. (The cabbages, not Melnick's head.)
- 2 tablespoons kosher salt

What you'll need to make it:

- Large mixing bowl. Because the best place to mix something is in a bowl meant for mixing.
- Sauerkraut crock.

- Wooden spoon, like the big one my aunt Meema hit me with when her false teeth fell out of her mouth and landed in the goulash.
- Clear the kitchen. This stuff doesn't always smell like roses.

How you should make it, so give a listen:

1. You *smoosh* the cabbage and salt together in your mixing bowl. Make sure your hands are clean, because you don't know where they've been! Squeeze the cabbage and salt together with your hands, but do it nice because cabbages have feelings, too.

2. The cabbage should become limp like Epstein the Tailor's shirt collars in August. You should have lots of cabbage juice. Put the whole schmear into a sauerkraut crock. *Smoosh* the salted cabbage into the crock good and tight as you can, and make sure there are no bubbles, until it is drowning in the liquid. Cover it up, but not too tight—the cabbage needs air to ferment properly—and then let it sit and mind its own business at room temperature for at least a week. You can even let it sit for a month almost. Try some sauerkraut every few days, until it makes you happy. And if you're like most of my friends, you're never happy. Then put it someplace where it's cold. You do that, and it will keep for six months. Of course, the idea is to nosh on it, so why would you keep it for six months?

3. Follow my instructions, and you'll have a nice two quarts.

A warning: When you serve the sauerkraut in your apartment to more than three people, like for a dinner or a lunch, open all the windows as wide as you can one hour after eating. Sauerkraut is delicious, but it's the gift that keeps on giving, if you know what I mean.